'Spoilspor ... is eyes traile ... - draped for

Cindy groaned and frantically leaned forward to try and cover where the wayward sheet had been pulled away from her hips. The heat that she knew must have turned her face bright red spread rapidly through her at the look on his face.

'Will you get the hell out of my bedroom?' Cindy managed in a near shriek.

'Correction, sweetheart, it's actually *my* bedroom. But I did knock a couple of times.'

The husky, laughter-choked murmur sent shivers straight down Cindy's spine. She gaped at him. The scowling, arrogant man of the evening before was utterly transformed.

Kids. . .one of life's joys, one of life's treasures.

Kisses. . .of warmth, kisses of passion, kisses from mothers and kisses from lovers.

In ***Kids & Kisses***. . .every story has it all.

Mary Hawkins lives with her minister husband and two of their three grown children in the Hunter Valley north of Sydney, but still thinks of herself as a Queenslander! She is a registered nurse who returned to her profession several years ago after a long break and found tremendous changes in the medical world. Now her love of nursing has been surpassed by her love of writing, but close contacts in the medical profession help keep her stories current and real to life.

Recent titles by the same author:

TRUSTING DR SCOTT

SUNSHINE REMEDY

BY

MARY HAWKINS

MILLS & BOON®

All the characters in this book have no existence outside the imagination of the author, and have no relation whatsoever to anyone bearing the same name or names. They are not even distantly inspired by any individual known or unknown to the author, and all the incidents are pure invention.

First published in Great Britain 1997
Harlequin Mills & Boon Limited,
Eton House, 18-24 Paradise Road, Richmond, Surrey TW9 1SR

ISBN 0 263 80639 1

Set in Times 10 on 11 pt. by
Rowland Phototypesetting Limited
Bury St Edmunds, Suffolk

03-9802-50035-D

Printed and bound in Great Britain
by Mackays of Chatham PLC, Chatham

CHAPTER ONE

THE streaker racing through the open gate was male.

Definitely male.

His lack of clothing confirmed it even if his gleeful face, dark amber eyes and gorgeous bouncing black curls could have belonged to either gender.

For a moment he grinned across at Cindy and then continued his rush across the grassy footpath to the road.

'Whoa, young man! Where are you going in such a hurry?'

Cindy dropped her street map and leapt forward, just managing to grab him by the arm as he reached the bitumen. At the same time there was a shriek of brakes and a car went whizzing by. An irate teenager yelled something at them and then the car was gone with an extra burst of speed.

'Car!' the small cherub shouted gleefully.

'Yes, a car,' Cindy said grimly, looking down at the toddler. 'A car going much too fast on this road, and one that would have squashed you flat, young man.'

At her cross voice the twinkle disappeared from the flashing eyes. She forced a smile at him, and instantly he grinned wickedly back at her.

'I's hiding.'

'Are you just, you little villain? Well, it's much safer hiding in your own yard than on this road.'

He suddenly tried to tug away and her grip on him tightened. The small face twisted into a scowl, the dark eyes glaring at her.

'Le' go!' he demanded in no uncertain tones.

'Not on your sweet life,' Cindy said cheerfully.

She studied his stormy face for a wistful moment. Always hidden in Cindy's heart had been the desire for a family of her own. She estimated he must still be under two years old, but already he was tall and had all the expressive dark eyes, dark hair and clear olive skin that could one day make a genuine tall, dark and handsome hunk. And she had always been a sucker for them.

He still strained away from Cindy as she said, 'Let's find your mother instead.'

To her dismay the small face crumpled. 'Can't. Mummy's gone,' he wailed loudly.

'Will!' A small tornado erupted from the same open gate and raced towards them.

The hand in Cindy's tried to pull free again, and this time she let him go. Immediately he was hauled up awkwardly into the arms of a small girl with similar black curly hair and dark eyes.

'What did you do to him?' The dark eyes flashed accusingly. 'He's crying.'

Cindy straightened. 'Stopped him running out in front of a car. Where's your mother?'

The dark eyes went even darker, and Cindy noticed she looked as though she had been crying recently.

'None of your business.' The girl scowled and turned away.

Cindy frowned at her rudeness and for a moment watched her march away. With a wry smile twisting her face, she turned back to continue checking the street instructions her brother had roughly mapped for her to help her find Dr Andrew Sack's house. There she had been assured she could pick up the key to her new flat which was, apparently, nearby. But her eyes were drawn back to the young girl, gallantly hanging onto a rebellious, wriggling boy.

'Down!' she heard him yell, and the girl's answer was muffled.

Cindy hesitated. As rude as the young madam was, she was still right. It was none of her business. She should be finding her flat so she could have a quick look to make sure her furniture and crates had arrived safely. Then it would be time to go back to the beach and try and prise Naomi away from her friends she had unexpectedly found. Her sister-in-law would be in a flap if they arrived back too late at the farm, having to drive in the dark on that last stretch of winding, narrow road.

But, then, too many young children from the area surrounding the last general practice where she had been working had been left to fend for themselves during the day.

Just as the girl and her burden almost reached the open gate in the high picket fence another girl, younger still, ran out. 'Brit,' she called urgently, 'he's getting madder and madder. Will, you're a naughty, naughty boy!' she scolded.

So there was an adult home. Cindy frowned. Mother gone and 'he' was angry.

She started forward after the children and at the same moment a furious male voice bellowed from the house a few metres away, 'Brittany! Susan! Where *are* you kids?'

Cindy quickened her pace and was just behind the children at the bottom of a couple of steps when a tall man came out on the small front patio of the sprawling brick house. He was holding a small mobile phone to his ear. She saw him speak into it rapidly and then close it up before he turned.

Dark eyes collided with her blue ones. They widened and swept over her long, tousled blonde hair, down over the unbuttoned blouse that covered her sandy, still damp, red bikini and merely brushed the top of her long bare legs.

He was the grown-up version of the toddler, only where the baby face had been plump and dimpled his was firmly masculine with a strong jaw and a nose that was a little too prominent. But the same dark curls of the miniature male framed a wide forehead and penetrating eyes.

Too penetrating.

A shiver swept through Cindy as he stared steadily at her.

The man was very tall, probably even taller than her twin brother, Casey, and he was over six feet. The T-shirt clinging to broad shoulders tapered to a pair of slim hips covered by tailored shorts. In fact, he was the most impressive man she'd seen for a long, long time.

No, impressive was the wrong word. Stunning. He was simply stunning.

Suddenly he strode forward and what was left of Cindy's mind went haywire. His moving body was poetry in motion. Muscular motion.

A little dazed, Cindy thought, He. . .he's built like a front row forward, and then was jolted to her senses by the harsh words that were being flung towards. . .yes, straight over the children's heads and towards *her*!

'Well, so you've deigned to turn up at last? Two hours! Two hours I've been waiting!' he accused her savagely.

Cindy suddenly knew what it felt like to literally have her mouth drop open. The eyes that had swept appreciatively over her body had hardened to a cold glare. Before she could gather her scattered wits the man turned on the children, who had taken the opportunity to try and slip past him.

'I'll find out later who left that gate open, Brittany,' he said very sternly. The older girl flushed and then hung her head. 'Now, get these two bathed and ready for their tea, and perhaps—'

He swung back to Cindy. His face was not only filled with wrath but, as his gaze swept over her again, was so filled with contempt that Cindy found her hands trying to pull the front pieces of her blouse together.

'Perhaps now this. . .this *lady* has at last finished her time at the beach she'll do what we were told she would do and cook us all some tea.' His voice was heavy with anger and scathing contempt. 'You're much younger than I thought, but that's no excuse. Aileen said she asked you to come immediately! And don't you know the risks of melanoma, allowing yourself to get so sunburnt?'

'Of course I know the risks of—' Cindy put a hand to her mouth. What else had he said? she thought in a daze. Come immediately, wasn't it? And. . .and. . .

'Cook you some tea?' she said faintly.

The man had already swung away, but he turned back with a groan. 'Don't tell me you can't even cook?' he growled furiously.

'Of course I can cook,' Cindy was stung into flinging back at him.

'Good!' he snapped, and before she could say another word he disappeared into the house.

Cindy took a deep, deep breath. Just as well she'd followed her instinct and chased after the children to make sure they would be all right. The man was obviously quite, quite mad! Of course, what she should do was head straight back to her car.

She was still telling herself that as she stepped up onto the veranda and reached out to open the screen door which had slammed behind the tall figure. It flew open, and she took a hasty step back.

Dark eyes glared at her again as he brushed past her. 'I don't know how long I'll be,' he snapped. 'Could be a couple of hours, even longer if I get any more house calls. I should be home for the kids' bedtime. If not, Susan and Will go to bed at seven and, seeing it's Sunday, even though tomorrow is a school day Brittany can stay up until I get home.'

House calls? Cindy noticed the black bag he was

carrying for the first time. She had been told there was only one medical centre in the small town of Sandy Beach. The two doctors who were partners there she had met at her interview. Dr Burston was due to retire and the other was his son-in-law, Andrew Sack.

A dreadful suspicion leapt into her mind about who this man must be. But who on earth did he think she was? Unless, of course, he knew and just expected the new doctor to act as babysitter, cook and anything else he needed!

He had reached the bottom of the short flight of steps before Cindy found her voice. 'You're leaving? Just like that?'

'I should have been gone two hours ago!' he flung back over his shoulder without a pause in the long strides that were taking him across to a sleek black car.

'But the children? Is anyone home with them?' she called after him.

'You are!'

The exasperated words were flung at her again, without him pausing. He bent to put his key in the car door, and Cindy knew with horrible certainty that in a moment he would be gone.

She put two fingers into her mouth and was proud of her piercing whistle. The tall figure straightened as though it had been shot. The dark head swung around. She barely suppressed a grin at the astounded look on the man's face. Even Casey would have envied that whistle!

Without a word he watched her advance towards him, his expression changing back to an autocratic frown.

'Let me get this straight,' Cindy said crisply. 'There's no other adult in the house with those children?'

He merely scowled even more and watched her coldly.

Indignation swept through Cindy. 'You're leaving a perfect stranger to stay with your children for. . .for who knows how long?'

He closed his eyes momentarily and took a deep breath. Then he looked at her.

'No, I am not leaving them with a perfect stranger,' he said in a tightly controlled voice. 'I'm leaving them with the woman Aileen told me my mother knows very well, and whom she employed before racing off to the hospital, and who should have been here ages ago to help out instead of gallivanting off to goodness knows where! Now, I've got four patients waiting for me.' He flung open his car door.

'What's your name?' Cindy managed from suddenly strangled vocal cords, knowing what he would say even as he said sharply, 'Daniel Burston, of course!'

Then he was in the car and Cindy watched helplessly as it backed down the driveway to finally disappear with a burst of speed.

Daniel Burston! Make that Dr Daniel Burston, son of the senior doctor of the practice she would be working in for the last six-month stint of her series of four six-monthly periods at different general practices, as required for her family medicine training to be a general practitioner. And hadn't Dr Burston senior said at her interview that he hoped his son would be joining the family practice, hopefully just after the end of her term with them but just as soon as he had sorted himself out? Whatever that had meant.

Well, obviously Daniel Burston had 'sorted himself out' sooner than anticipated.

Cindy's lips firmed as disappointment filled her. The body might be OK. All right, more than OK. The word was gorgeous, absolutely gorgeous, but what an arrogant, rude, impatient man. No doubt he'd be impossible to work with.

Her legs were trembling slightly as she slowly made her way into the house. As she let the front door close behind her pandemonium erupted from somewhere inside.

'I can too bath myself and I can so help with Will!' a small voice shrieked.

'Dad said for me to bath you both. Will, leave that soap alone!'

'Fwog!'

Cindy strode swiftly in the direction of the raised voices, and as she reached a large bathroom there was another roar.

'Mine fwog!'

'Is not, that's mine. You broke yours!'

The smallest of the two girls burst through the doorway of the bathroom and almost collided with Cindy. She was clutching a large green rubber frog.

'Hello,' Cindy said calmly. 'Are you Susan? What have you got there? Is that Kermit the Frog, one of the Muppets?'

The small girl stared at her and then nodded shyly.

There had been a sudden silence in the bathroom when Cindy started to speak. She moved past Susan and into the room. Brittany turned from where she was kneeling in a pool of water and glanced briefly up at her, before continuing to apply a facecloth vigorously to Will.

Cindy had been twelve years old when her long-awaited baby sister, Naomi, had arrived. But she had been absolutely thrilled to have a sister after three brothers, and still remembered how protective she had been of her ability to help her mother with the new arrival.

'Brittany? Is that your name?' Cindy waited patiently for the nod which was slow in coming. 'And this young rogue is Will. Did he get away from you just after you finished undressing him?' she said with a chuckle.

Brittany glanced up at her again, studied Cindy's face cautiously for a long moment and then her pretty face lit up. She giggled. 'Dad had just undressed him for me when the phone rang again. I answered it for him, but by the time he had come to talk to one of his patients and I got back to the bathroom Will had gone. But he did look funny, didn't he?'

Cindy laughed. 'It's not every day a handsome young man runs down the footpath like that towards me.'

Brittany giggled again, and then Susan joined in. Not to be left out, Will laughed, too, but his fists splashing up and down in the water got all their attention.

'Will!' Brittany yelled at him and moved quickly away. 'Now you've made me all wet.'

Cindy had thought Brittany was already liberally splashed, but she said cheerfully, 'Goodness, you're a little devil. Can I lift him out for you, Brittany?'

Brittany hesitated, but stood up and moved aside. 'Yes, please, he's awful slippery to get out sometimes.'

Another mark against the absent Dr Burston. He should never expect a child of Brittany's age to supervise his other children's baths like this even if their mother had been rushed to the hospital.

It was obviously a very touchy subject, by the reaction from Will and then Brittany, so she refrained from asking any of the questions tumbling through her mind. She thoughtfully watched Brittany dry the wriggling infant and then expertly start to put a disposable nappy on him.

Cindy glanced around the neat bathroom and then noticed the wide-eyed girl in the doorway still staring at her. She smiled at her gently, but the small figure clutched her frog even closer and scowled.

'Who are you?' Susan asked suddenly.

At last somebody wants to know, Cindy thought grimly, but before she could speak Brittany said, 'She's that lady who's a friend of Grandma's and promised to come when—' She stopped abruptly, glanced up at Cindy and quickly away again, but not before Cindy saw the tears start to whelm up again.

'I didn't know it was you when we were out on the footpath,' a slightly teary voice added apologetically.

Susan said indignantly, 'She's not Mrs Campbell. I've never seen her before ever.'

Brittany looked up sharply, stared at Susan and then suspiciously at Cindy. Cindy looked thoughtfully from one child to the other. Something wasn't quite right here. Why didn't Brittany know Mrs Campbell as well as her sister did?

'You're perfectly right, I'm not Mrs Campbell. My name's Cindy James, but I have been employed by your grandfather to work with him.'

Brittany's face cleared. 'Oh, you're Dr James!'

Cindy smiled at her gently. 'That's right,' she said cheerfully, thinking rapidly. She glanced at her watch, and came to a decision. After all, Daniel Burston said he could be away for two hours at least. There was no way she could leave these children by themselves and Naomi would soon be wondering where she had got to.

Brittany suddenly frowned up at her. 'Dad's been very, very cross with you because you've been sick and couldn't start work soon enough before the holidays. Are you better now?'

Cindy cringed inwardly. She already felt guilty and cross enough with herself for not being able to commence work when originally agreed.

She said slowly, 'I still get tired too quickly, but I'm almost better. I hope to start work next week.' Even if this time Casey still doesn't want me to, she refrained from adding out loud. 'Now,' she asked quickly, 'apparently it's almost your teatime?'

The trio watching her nodded vigorously.

'Do you like fish and chips?' She grinned at the chorus of approval. 'Well, I saw a take-away down near the beach where I left my sister. I've got to collect her so what about all coming with me to fetch her, and we'll have tea there?'

There was another clamour of approval, but Brittany suddenly looked doubtful. 'What about Dad? And. . .and we aren't allowed to go in a car with a stranger.'

'Good girl,' Cindy said warmly. 'I'm glad you've got so much sense. We'll leave a message for your dad in case he does come home early. And while I ring my sister-in-law to tell her what's happened would you like to run out to my car and get my bag? I'll show you my driver's licence. Would that do?'

Brittany was more than happy, and in a short while they had piled into the car, found an astounded but compliant Naomi on the beach and were soon seated on large beach towels on the sand, eating piping hot fish and chips.

Short work was made of the food. There was one tense moment which Naomi caused when she asked casually about their mother. Tears threatened again on all three children's faces.

Cindy gave her sister a warning look and said casually, 'Oh, apparently she's had to go to the hospital. Now, if you're all finished,' she added quickly, 'we've only got a few moments, but that foam from the spent waves is just asking to be played in for a little while.'

It only took a few moments for the incoming tide to trick all three children and the water to surge around and up small legs to wet their clothes. The older two looked a little apprehensively at Cindy the first time, but then laughed gleefully as she grinned at them.

Even Brittany was soon trying to stamp on the foam before it disappeared on the wet sand, but it wasn't long before she stopped and stood, watching Susan and Will chasing Naomi around in circles on the firm sand.

'What's wrong, Brittany?' Cindy asked gently.

She lifted a worried little face and said anxiously, 'We really shouldn't be here without Dad knowing, even if we did leave a note. I don't know if he left the answering service on, and. . .and there could be a call from the hospital.'

Brittany had informed them that she was eight, Susan was four and Will was still waiting for his second birthday. A pang caught Cindy unawares. Brittany seemed so much older for her age than most girls Cindy had come across, and condemnation filled her for the mother and father who expected so much of this sturdy child with such a strong sense of responsibility.

The child's mouth quivered so much that Cindy said hastily, 'Well, the sun will be down soon and it's getting colder already so we have to go anyway. Our young man here certainly needs another bath.'

Brittany had been right about the answering service not being switched on. Cindy was in the bathroom when the phone urgently summoned her. She had only just tossed off her throwover blouse to change into the clothes she had grabbed out of her car, but raced to answer it.

It was an irate call from a patient who was still waiting for a house call.

'Dr Burston said he'd be here more than an hour ago,' the wheezing, breathless woman complained.

Cindy had answered the phone in a small, comfortably furnished office, and took a few moments to reassure the elderly woman that the doctor had been unavoidably delayed but she was sure he would be with her soon.

She had just hung up the phone when it rang again. Cindy ruefully looked down at her scantily clad body. The air was cooler in here, too. At this rate she'd never get out of this bikini.

'My little girl's burning up and I can hardly wake her,' an hysterical woman's voice cried out.

Cindy managed to calm the woman enough to get her name and address, and then she asked quietly, 'How old is she, Mrs Owen, and when did you first notice she was sick?'

While she listened to the answer she unsuccessfully searched the desk for a phone book that might tell her Daniel Burston's mobile phone number.

'She's eighteen months old,' the tearful voice told her. 'She's been having a lovely time all day, running around on the beach, and not a sign of being sick until a couple of hours ago when she became irritable. She. . .she even vomited once, but now. . . At first I thought she was just sleepy, but she's burning up and—'

'Is she sunburnt at all?' Cindy interrupted quickly.

There was a pause, and then the woman said rapidly, 'We kept her shirt on for most of the day as it was so hot. We did put some cream on her but she. . .she is rather red on her arms and legs and face, though,' she added defensively.

Cindy closed her eyes and her lips tightened. All day at the beach! Her own long legs and white skin had been kissed by the sun too much after only a couple of hours in the afternoon when the strength of the ultraviolet rays was waning. How many foolish parents neglected to realise how hot the sun could be, even at the beginning of summer! A small child could dehydrate very quickly.

'Now, Mrs Owen, I want you to listen carefully. Your little girl probably has an infection of some kind, but it could also be heat exhaustion. Will she drink at all for you?'

Cindy wasn't surprised by the tearful, negative answer. She asked a few more questions and then said crisply, 'You have to try and force some fluid into her. Lemonade mixed with water is best, but get anything into her until I get there. Do you have any infant paracetamol syrup? You do? Good. Try and get her to swallow a teaspoonful. I'll get there as soon as I can, but I want you also to very quickly run a cool bath and—'

'Mrs Campbell! What the devil do you think you're doing!'

Cindy jumped violently at the furious, incredulous voice behind her. A large hand brushed against her bare shoulders as it reached over to grab the phone away from her.

CHAPTER TWO

CINDY spun around, deftly avoiding Daniel Burston's hand, and said rapidly, 'Just a moment, Mrs Owen. Dr Burston's just walked in.'

She covered the phone mouthpiece and hissed angrily, 'I am *not* Mrs Campbell. This is an hysterical mother with an eighteen-month-old baby who is sunburnt, very lethargic and PUO. Seemed well and happy *all day* at the beach. No cold or cough, no diarrhoea, diminished urinary output and not teething, as far as the mother knows. Has been irritable for the last couple of hours, sweating profusely but not as much now. Vomited once. Refusing fluids.

'It could be an infection, of course, but with the sunburn I suggest heat exhaustion at the very least, possibly verging on heatstroke.'

Cindy pointed to the details she had noted on the message pad and handed him the phone.

He stared at her with an arrested look on his face for a moment, and then gave his attention to the frantic caller. He started telling the woman to make sure she tried to cool the child down in the bath, as well as give her the medication and fluids, and he'd be there as soon as possible.

All the time he was talking his eyes swept over Cindy's curvaceous body, covered only by the scraps of material of the bikini. Inwardly Cindy cringed, wishing fervently she had not yielded to Susan's pleas to 'get with it, big sis.' Her own modest swimming costumes were still packed in one of the boxes in her flat so she had reluctantly ended up borrowing her sister's brief bikini.

Cindy had known she was still not strong enough to do battle with the surf, but she had been restless after first of all being confined to a hospital bed and then by all the cosseting at home. That restlessness had improved only a little during the last few days since Casey, who had always sensed her needs without being told, had arrived unexpectedly at her parents' home a week ago to rescue her.

Her mother had reluctantly agreed to her going to stay with him and his pregnant wife, Kim, but only if Naomi went too. Having just finished her higher school certificate and left school early before the official start to the long summer school holidays, the teenager had been thrilled. For the last few days she had proved to be an invaluable help around the house and with her small niece and nephew. Unfortunately, that had left Kim too much time to fuss over Cindy. Today it had been good to escape, despite her protests.

Cindy's pale skin, now flushed pink by the sun, was proof that it had been years since she had even visited a swimming pool. Being only an hour's drive from the sea had been irresistible, and she had donned the bikini amid much teasing from Susan and her jealous sister-in-law who bemoaned her own lost waistline.

She had discovered that the drive from her brother's farm had tired her much more than she had expected, and her skin had been far too pale to do more than paddle briefly and lie on a beach towel in the shade. She had fallen into a deep sleep and, unfortunately, by the time she woke the sun had moved so that her face and shoulders had been exposed to too much sun.

After a thorough inspection of her slim, tall body Daniel's eyes drifted over her windblown, fluffy blonde hair that tumbled around her shoulders, and fastened for a moment on Cindy's face before he again inspected the now thoroughly heated body bearing his scrutiny with deep embarrassment.

Suddenly Cindy felt far more exposed in her skimpy bikini here in this small room than she ever had on the beach. But she stood her ground, hoping he would mistake the hot flush for sun burn. Not for a moment did she look away from his piercing eyes when they at last returned to hers.

Suddenly her sense of humour kicked in. It swept away her self-consciousness and a grin twitched her lips.

Daniel's eyebrows shot up and she turned away abruptly so he could not see her face. He was angry enough, without her amusement infuriating him further. Her sense of the ridiculous had many times got her into trouble and this time it chased away the anger his abrupt actions had caused.

The poor man! What doctor would like to walk in on a bright red bikini-clad, blonde bimbo, taking a professional call from a patient and handing out medical treatment over the phone?

Then the laughter that had whelmed up died away. And what kind of a man was a doctor who would leave his children with a complete stranger, without asking even the most basic questions?

'I was told Mrs Campbell was not too old, tall and blonde,' a sharp voice said behind Cindy.

Not too old! Cindy swung round and glared back at him.

'I am Cindy James,' she said with all the dignity she could muster. '*Dr* Cindy James.'

His dark eyes swept her from head to toe again. The disbelief that filled his face made her so angry she went on the attack.

'If you didn't even know Mrs Campbell what kind of father are you to leave your children with a perfect stranger?'

Something flickered in his eyes. Cindy thought she saw a fleeting look of pain, and relented.

'They're all perfectly OK,' she added rapidly. 'We had fish and chips and played on the beach until Brittany became worried about not being home in case your wife rang.'

He stood very still for such a long moment that Cindy tensed.

'My wife?'

The confusion and pain that strangled his voice melted Cindy's anger completely. 'Look, I'm sure she must be all right or the hospital would have rung,' she said compassionately.

'She's not all right. She's dead.'

Cindy stared at him. The bleakness in his face stunned her even more. He held her horrified gaze for a moment and then closed his eyes briefly and shook his head.

'Look,' he said harshly, 'I haven't got a clue what you're on about and there's no time to fill you in now. I had to come past here on the way to my next patient and wanted to make sure you were managing all right, or rather that Mrs Campbell was managing all right. I take it she's putting the children to bed.'

It was a statement, not a query, and—not waiting for an answer—he turned abruptly away and started for the door. 'Baby Owen can't wait. I'll be back as soon as possible.'

Cindy gave a startled protest and he swung back. 'Dr James, don't you dare mention her mother to Brittany. She'll get too upset.'

His gaze swept over her again. This time it was scathing!

'And if you're well enough to go surfing, surely you could have started work sooner. If you had been here working as originally planned this hell of a day would not have been anywhere near as bad! Now you're here

I expect you to help out in this crisis.'

She was still standing frozen to the spot when she heard the front door slam.

'I couldn't help getting the flu and then pneumonia,' she muttered out loud at last.

And she had really not been able to help being so run-down from overwork that it had taken her the last three weeks to recover, instead of starting work here when she had been scheduled to two weeks ago.

And now this poor man's wife had died. Did his children know? They obviously knew something was wrong, Brittany especially.

But nothing made sense. Where was his father and Andrew Sack? When had his wife died? Aileen, he had called her. If it had been today surely he would have been more upset and he would certainly not still be working.

The phone pealed out its summons again, and Cindy automatically reached for it. 'Dr James speaking.'

There was a brief pause and then a distressed woman's voice exclaimed, 'Dr James? Oh, no! In all the turmoil of going to the hospital I forgot all about you coming to get your key this afternoon! I do hope Dan has been able to find it for you. And I'm *so* pleased you've arrived and have stayed on after all. Dan must be relieved to have help.'

Cindy interrupted the rapid flow as soon as she could. 'Who is speaking, please?'

'I'm Dan's sister, Aileen Sack.'

In a daze Cindy registered that the mother, Aileen, who had gone to the hospital was Dr Burston's sister, *not* wife.

'I believe you met my husband, Andrew, when you came to look at the practice a few months ago. I was so sorry I was away,' the woman was saying very quickly. 'I just rang to let everyone know that Andrew's all right at the moment, and to make sure the kids are OK. Poor little ones, they were so scared.

'Please don't tell them, and Daniel will no doubt ring here as soon as he can, but the ultrasound confirmed that it's gallstones and one is still. . .still. . .'

Her voice faltered for a moment and then she continued in a rush, 'He's still in so much pain they are trying to organise for Andrew to have his gall bladder out tomorrow and want to keep him in hospital overnight. I do hope Mrs Campbell can stay tomorrow as well.'

There was the sound of a sharp voice in the background.

'Oh, dear, Sister let me ring from this ward phone but now she needs it. I'll ring again in the morning.'

The rushed words stopped abruptly and the dialling tone sounded. Cindy slowly took the receiver away from her ear and looked at it blankly, before slowly hanging it up.

What was it with this brother and sister? she thought crossly. They never finished a conversation properly!

Poor Andrew Sack. So he was the 'crisis'. He had obviously been rushed to hospital with acute cholecystitis. Cindy had been told that the nearest hospital to Sandy Cove was well over an hour's travel away, but if they wanted to operate immediately it must be a bad bout.

So that explained where one doctor was. Where was the senior Dr Burston? A feeling of relief swept through her. At least Daniel Burston's wife must have died some time ago. Perhaps his children were just being looked after by his sister.

'One question answered—a few more to go,' Cindy said grimly, and grabbed the phone irritably as it rang again.

Another question answered. Mrs Campbell's car had broken down on the trip in from her farm. She had waited for ages, hoping to get a lift, but had ended up having to walk miles back to her home.

'I'm dreadfully sorry, Dr James,' the slightly out-of-breath voice said urgently. 'My husband does all the repairs himself and he won't be home for another few days. He'd be very angry if I tried to get anyone else to repair his precious car. I'm dreadfully sorry to let her down, but Aileen will just have to get someone else to live in and mind the children.'

When she had concluded the call Cindy stood thoughtfully for a moment. Then she sighed, knowing she really had no choice, and picked up the phone to dial Casey's number. She was thankful it was her brother who answered and not his over-protective wife.

Casey accepted her hurried explanations calmly, merely adding the caution, 'Just you make sure you let Naomi do the running around. You haven't even finished that last course of antibiotics yet. Remember the doctor said you'd have to take life much slower for quite a while still.'

Cindy had no need of the caution. Already she was beginning to feel the effects of the day and especially the tension of the last hour or more. As she went in search of Naomi she silently cursed her weakness.

She smiled at the scene that met her in the kitchen. Naomi had put her skills as chief babysitter of nephews and nieces in their large family to good use. Even Brittany was in her pyjamas, sitting at the table with the other two, while Naomi poured out glasses of fruit juice.

'Your dad only popped in for a moment to make sure you were all OK.' Cindy smiled at Brittany as her eyes lit up, and added quickly, 'He had to go out again on an emergency, but your aunt rang and Mrs Campbell, too.'

She told them quickly what had been said and then added, with a warning look at Naomi, 'So it looks like

Naomi and I will be sleeping here in case your dad is called out during the night.'

She was thankful Naomi's astonished frown subsided to a resigned grimace. But Susan's face suddenly crumpled. Will let out a sudden roar. 'Want my Mummy and Daddy!' He then burst into noisy sobs.

Brittany jumped up, but Naomi already had him in her arms. There was such a look of misery on the face Brittany turned towards Cindy that she bent to give her a tender hug. The tense little body pulled away sharply and Cindy reluctantly let her hands fall.

Keeping her face down, Brittany pushed her chair back and said in a choked voice before she bolted out of the room, 'It's time they were in bed.'

It took some time to stop the tears and settle the two small children in their beds. By the time the last story had been told and the lights were out Cindy felt her body beginning to tremble with exhaustion. As she walked down the hallway to the kitchen a spasm of coughing shook her.

There were so many questions she had intended to ask Brittany but she subsided into a chair and looked at Naomi's concerned face helplessly. She had already managed to speak to her for a few moments, telling her she had rung Casey.

'Right, Brittany,' Naomi said briskly. 'Where do we sleep for the night?' She grinned at Cindy. 'It's time to put my big sis to bed now.'

Brittany looked at Cindy from her own strained little face and her eyes widened. 'You look awful white.'

'Just tired, love,' Cindy assured her quickly. 'Today's been the first time I've even driven my car since I first became sick, and it's taking me longer than I thought to get strong again. Getting a bit sunburnt hasn't helped either, I'm afraid,' she added ruefully. 'I know it's still early but I just need a good night's sleep and I'll be fine.'

There was a hurried consultation between Naomi and Brittany, but Cindy relaxed and closed her eyes. She didn't care how the beds were organised as long as she could lie down very soon.

At last, at Naomi's urging, she wasted no time having a sketchy shower to rid her body of sand and sea, before tumbling thankfully onto the bed Naomi led her to in a pleasant little room. It was still quite warm and she didn't even bother getting into the nightgown Brittany had placed ready for her.

With a sigh of relief she pulled the bedclothes over herself. For some ridiculous reason her last conscious thought was that she should really be feeling guilty for the relief which had swept through her when she had realised that Daniel Burston was no longer married, and in a matter of seconds she was sound asleep.

It was sunshine, suddenly released into the bedroom and allowed to shine right onto her face, that woke her. She threw up an arm for protection and groaned, then flung herself over to burrow her head again in the pillow away from the offending light.

Someone loudly cleared a throat. 'Don't you want your cup of coffee, Dr James?' a loud masculine voice accused mildly.

Cindy sat bolt upright. Her startled eyes looked straight into laughter-filled, warm brown ones only a few inches away. The eyes slipped lower and lingered appreciatively. Cindy glanced down at herself and gasped. Some time in the night the blanket had disappeared completely. The sheet barely covered her from the waist down. The rest of her generous curves were on full view.

She frantically yanked up the sheet to her chin and glared at Daniel.

'Spoilsport,' he muttered as his eyes trailed down over her sheet-draped form.

As Cindy glared at him the cup in his large hand tilted alarmingly. He gave a strangled sound and her eyes flew to where his had landed.

She groaned and said a very unladylike word. Frantically she leaned forward and tried to cover where the wayward sheet had been pulled away from her hips. Naturally it then slithered away from her breasts. Abruptly she twisted the sheet around her tightly and fell back on the pillow.

The heat that she knew must have turned her face bright red spread rapidly through her at the look on his face.

'Will you get the hell out of my bedroom?' she managed in a near shriek.

'Correction, sweetheart, it's actually *my* bedroom. But I did knock a couple of times.'

The husky, laughter-choked murmur sent shivers straight down Cindy's spine. She gaped at him. The scowling, arrogant man of the evening before was utterly transformed.

He was dressed more formally in a shirt and tie, but his curly black hair was attractively tousled. Daniel Burston was simply a smiling, gorgeous man that dreams were made of. Or at least, she told herself hurriedly, any susceptible woman with any brains at all would think so.

He was still leisurely studying her long length, now closely moulded by the thin polyester sheet. His eyes lingered on her generous breasts. Her nipples tingled and Cindy's body started to burn. Indignation stirred at his blatant, appreciative survey.

Very carefully making sure she remained decently covered, she sat up again and raised her chin.

'Like what you see?'

She stared coldly back at him when his eyes swung to her face. Surprise gleamed for a moment and then they filled with such a warm, teasing light that Cindy felt her heart turn completely over. Her own indignation at his intrusion of her privacy began to fade rapidly.

'Very much, thank you,' he said very politely, 'although I liked the first view much better.'

Cindy promptly lost the battle to stop the heat again staining her face red.

While her senses were still scattered he continued blandly, as though they were merely discussing the weather, 'I did think of sneaking in and just grabbing my change of clothes, but I thought you might appreciate speaking to me before I raced off again and disappeared for the morning.'

Cindy found her voice as he paused. 'You are certainly not racing off anywhere until we get a few things straight,' she started indignantly.

He raised those thick, coal-black eyebrows and widened his eyes in mock acknowledgement. That gleam of amusement shone briefly again at her. Something inside Cindy responded in a manner that confused her. She wasn't sure she liked the feeling one scrap. No one had ever had this weird effect on her before.

'We certainly had our wires crossed yesterday,' his deep, mellow voice said. 'Last night Brittany had given up on me and gone to bed, but Naomi filled me in on what happened to Mrs Campbell. She also gave me a stern lecture about her sister still recovering from her serious illness, if you call flu and a chest infection serious. Very protective of her "big sis", isn't she?'

Cindy was still trying to come to grips with the effect his voice and closeness was having on her, and couldn't think of a word to say before he continued in even tones, 'If you'd prefer, I could let you stay here in my bed and return later to continue where we leave off.'

The sexual innuendo was blatant. His eyelids drooped and his gaze started to drift down her body again. Cindy felt that strange heat sweep through her body once more.

Suddenly she was conscious that her breasts had become heavy, and something stirred in the pit of her stomach.

She almost cried out, But we haven't even started yet.

'Er. . .that might be better,' she heard herself say in a husky voice that didn't sound anything like her usual one, and only then realised what she had said as his gaze suddenly scorched her.

For a moment all breath left her. His eyes darkened and something she could not read changed his expression. Tension filled the very air between them.

Suddenly desperately feeling the need for more air, she sucked in a breath and squeaked, 'I mean I. . . I. . .I'll talk to you later when I'm dressed.'

For a moment he did not move. Then he suddenly looked down at the forgotten cup in his hand. 'This will be getting too cold,' he said huskily. Abruptly he moved and set it down on the bedside cabinet. 'I'm leaving soon for the hospital and you'll have to start the morning surgery so get a move on,' he added abruptly.

Cindy wasted a full minute staring at the door he had gently closed behind him.

At last she drew a deep, deep breath. What had happened here?

She had never had a serious relationship with a man. Overprotective brothers in her teens and then the rigorous life first of a med student and then hospital residency had meant dates had been few and far between.

Perhaps more because she had never met a man who affected her like this before, she thought suddenly and honestly.

She glanced quickly around the room, seeing for the first time the evidence of a man's occupation. And then she wondered where he had slept. Had he perhaps wandered into his bedroom before talking to Naomi? And what had he thought if he had seen. . .?

Then she saw the time on a clock radio and groaned.

The sun must be barely up! Didn't the man ever sleep?

Cindy flung the sheet back and hurriedly stood up. For heaven's sake, she was a doctor! So was he! They saw naked bodies all the time. But there had been nothing of the doctor in the gaze that had swept over her body. That searing look had only held pure masculine appreciation of a woman and her body had responded as it never had before.

'And he looked pretty good himself,' Cindy muttered out loud.

And she thought he looked even better than ever when she rushed into the kitchen a few minutes later and found him seated at the table, pouring himself a cup of tea, a pile of toast in front of him.

'Mmm,' he murmured, after staring at her for a moment. 'I was beginning to wonder if you ever covered that delicious body of yours—when on your feet, that is.' His voice lowered still further to a very sensuous whisper. 'I didn't realise my old dressing-gown had so many curves.'

Cindy gulped. Desperately she tried to pull her professional mantle around her.

'Dr Burston! What. . .what did you mean, I'll have to take surgery?' she demanded abruptly. 'And where's Dr Burston, and what are you doing here?'

Daniel reached for a tub of margarine and began to quickly spread some on a piece of toast. 'Now that was a little confusing.' He looked up at Cindy and suddenly grinned. 'As this one's right here, I take it you mean where's the Dr Burston you met at your interview?'

Cindy watched helplessly as one well-shaped, tanned hand lifted the piece of toast to *very* well-shaped lips. Lips that would be flavoured as sweet as the honey he had just. . .

'As soon as she found out I'd sold my practice in Sydney my mother went on strike. She vowed there was no way she would tolerate another Christmas holiday tourist season in Sandy Cove, with Dad working all hours.'

A set of strong white teeth bit into the crisp toast. 'So Mum and Dad are somewhere between here and Melbourne. I did ring last night to where they said they might be staying to let them know about Andrew. But they hadn't arrived.'

Cindy had never realised how sexy a man's strong, tanned throat could be as the muscles moved when he swallowed food.

'Dr James, are you listening to me?'

The censorious tones brought Cindy's eyes flying back to his face. He was frowning at her impatiently.

'For goodness' sake sit down,' he suddenly barked at her. 'Don't tell me you're another woman who can't concentrate until she's had several cups of coffee and been awake for hours!'

As she thankfully collapsed onto the chair he indicated she frantically tried to pull that professional mantle around her as she had so pitifully failed to do before.

'I don't drink coffee.'

Daniel muttered something under his breath, and pulled a cup towards him. He poured her a cup of tea and handed it to her. Cindy was proud of the fact that as she took it from him her hand did not tremble. Quickly she helped herself to milk and a double dose of sugar, before taking a long, welcoming sip of the strong brew.

'I'm sorry I haven't time to get you any breakfast,' Daniel said abruptly. 'I only have a few minutes myself. As I was saying, I'm now your boss. In fact, I'll be your one and only while Andrew is out of action. There was pandemonium here yesterday when he developed severe abdo pain.'

'Cholecystitis. Your sister rang.'

A gentle smile tilted his lips briefly. 'So Naomi told

me. My dear sister is not noted for her calm when anyone she loves is sick. And Andrew was very sick yesterday. There was no way I could stop her going in the ambulance with him. And that's one reason I have to leave now. She needs me.'

He had added the last as though it was perfectly normal and natural to be there for his sister when she needed him. Sure, yesterday he'd had no choice. There had been no way he could have left his patients unattended. But now. . .

Cindy warmed towards him. Her own large family with all their differing personalities and varying interests always had as a matter of course put loved ones first. But she had learnt over the years not to take for granted that other families were the same.

'Are the gallstones blocking the common duct as well?' Cindy asked quietly.

Worry creased Daniel's forehead. 'Yes,' he said briefly. 'It's worse than we thought yesterday. The tests show he's one of the small percentage who also has pancreatitis. He's being operated on this morning and Aileen wants me there.' He hesitated. 'There's no need for the children to know.'

It was no more than Cindy had already worked out the evening before. Andrew Sack was very ill and, no doubt, would need some time to recover, which meant. . .

Daniel glanced at his watch, drained the last of his drink quickly and stood up. He pushed a bundle of keys across the table to Cindy.

'These are yours. There's a locked gate in the back fance that opens onto the medical centre. Saves us a much longer walk around the block. Surgery starts at eight and fortunately our other receptionist, Jennifer, was rostered on this morning instead of Aileen. She'll have to show you the ropes. Afraid I've got to run as soon as I've seen the kids.'

He was about to disappear on her yet again! Cindy put her cup down quickly. 'But what about me?'

His eyes narrowed. 'What about you?'

She hesitated. How could she tell him she was afraid of her confounded weakness, that she was afraid she would not be able to cope with uncomplicated surgery patients, let alone any emergency that cropped up, and that she desperately hoped he would not be gone all day? Obviously when they had been notified of her illness it must have been in the early stages before her condition had worsened, and he had no idea how ill she had really been.

Inwardly she gave a shrug. Well, there was no sense or time in worrying him about her now when he had no choice but to go. So, instead, she said quickly, 'I still have to be supervised. I know that this is an accredited practice for me to work in these next six months for me to gain my registration as a GP, but without either Dr Sack or your father. . . I understood him to say he wouldn't be retiring for the six months I was here. Doesn't his retiring alter the status of the practice?'

Daniel looked at her for a moment, the smile on his face completely gone. Cindy suddenly wanted to know what she had said to make the pleasant look on his face disappear so rapidly. He had not moved, but she knew suddenly that he had withdrawn from her.

And she wondered with a catch of breath why that suddenly mattered so much.

CHAPTER THREE

'YOU don't have to worry, Dr James. Your career will not suffer in the slightest. Dad hasn't officially retired yet.'

Daniel's voice was remote, as though he resented her in some way. Cindy straightened. Was he critical of her because she was concerned about her career?

'He's just taken an extended holiday, which he badly needs for his health,' Daniel continued sharply, 'although I would not be at all surprised if Mum has her way and they don't return for longer than the expected two months.'

He abruptly, almost angrily, pushed his chair in. 'You don't have to worry about your career. Dad already has let the powers that be know. My practice in Sydney was also accredited, and I'm registered as a supervisor so you'll have to make do with me.'

Before Cindy could respond he added abruptly, 'I intended to show you the set-up before I head off to the hospital to see what's happening to Andrew and Baby Owen, whom I had to admit to hospital last night.'

His voice softened a little. 'By the way, you were right. It was heatstroke. Poor little kid was as red as a lobster with sunburn. But I've run out of time now. The holiday-makers have already started to invade the place, and there's only you and me. With some luck, most of them will opt to stay well today. If not, you'll just have to cope.'

The protest that had flown to Cindy's lips died unuttered. He must have been given the message last week that her doctors had insisted she have at least another week, possibly two, off, before commencing any work at all. But if the town was left without any medical help how could she refuse to stay?

After the way she had felt so exhausted last night, she just had to hope and pray there were no emergencies she would not be strong enough to handle. There were still so many questions Cindy needed answered. But the sudden lack of friendliness in his abrupt voice made the questions slide away.

Her mind racing, she watched him as he gathered up his dirty plates and deposited them in the sink.

'But I. . .I don't even have my clothes here.'

If anything, his expression grew colder as it swept over her. 'That's already taken care of. Naomi gave me your brother's phone number and he assured me your things will be brought here this morning as soon as he's finished the milking.'

Cindy came to her feet. 'You've rung Casey already?'

'I rang him last night after talking to your sister.'

'And he agreed to me starting work?'

Daniel scowled at her. 'No, he didn't. He said you weren't well enough yet. However, Naomi then said she didn't mind staying to help look after the children and keep an eye on you, and he reluctantly agreed to bring in your things. But surely you don't need his permission! Your family's rather over-protective of you, I should think. You're a bit skinny but you seemed fine to me last night.'

Skinny! Cindy's eyes narrowed.

His voice had been expressionless, but she suddenly caught a fleeting gleam in his eyes which stopped the hostile words that had flown to her lips. Relief swept through her in a wave. Whatever had swept away his warmth towards her and triggered off his remote, professional attitude seemed to have been replaced, she fervently hoped for good, by that tendency to tease and provoke her.

Should she let him get away with the embarrassment he had subjected her to this morning? After all, he was her boss. They had to work together professionally.

Suddenly she threw caution to the winds. She pressed her lips together tightly as years of experience with three brothers older than herself rose to her assistance.

She looked down at her very unglamorous attire and gestured helplessly. Then she raised her eyes, managed a trembling smile that she had used very effectively numerous times over the years on tormenting siblings, and said with the deepest sigh she could, 'I'm sorry you think I look so unattractive.'

She let the tears whelm up and felt gleeful satisfaction at the startled look that swept over his face.

'I've been so sick, and the doctors did wonder if I might not have myalgic encephalomyelitis. But I'm sure I'll survive,' she added in a brave voice. 'I suppose if a patient arrives before Casey does I'll just have to go and climb into my bikini again. I'm certainly not going anywhere like this!'

Daniel stared at her suspiciously. She continued to look as pathetic as she could, but then her pose collapsed as Daniel threw back his head and roared with laughter. So he wasn't as easy to take in as most men were by her put-ons. Her own lips twitched, and then she was chuckling, too.

Then as they stared at each other the laughter died away. An electrical current leapt across the room between them.

Cindy's breathing quickened. Suddenly she felt as though she had known this man for years. Even though he might think she was malingering, even though he had seemed to withdraw himself from her a few minutes ago, he did share her sense of the ridiculous.

He took a couple of steps towards her, his eyes suddenly very serious. 'I certainly hope you don't have chronic fatigue syndrome, Cindy James, because I need you too much.'

Cindy tried to still the trembling that had started up deep inside her. Her head told her he needed her expertise as a doctor, but her wayward senses were telling her he really meant something entirely different.

'Dad, what were you laughing at?'

Brittany was standing in the doorway, staring from one to the other suspiciously.

Daniel moved forward and swung her up in his arms. 'Sorry, sweetheart, did I wake you up? Oh, dear, and not only you,' he added ruefully as two more little figures scampered into the room. 'Sorry, Dr James, I thought you might get a bit of peace before this mob descended on us.'

Brittany giggled as he swung her around, before putting her down and reaching to hug Susan briefly. Then he picked up the curly-headed toddler so like himself.

'Why do you call her Dr James, Dad? She told us to call her Cindy,' Brittany asked.

'Did she just? Right, Cindy it is, then, and she must call me Daniel, I suppose.'

'I won't if you prefer Dr Burston,' Cindy snapped, hurt at the reluctance in his voice, and then was completely disarmed at the smile he gave her.

She found herself smiling back at him with delight.

Brittany moved forward suddenly and slipped her hand into Daniel's. To Cindy's sudden dismay and confusion, she realised that Brittany was glaring at her as though she disliked her intensely.

Susan moved forward and said in an anxious little voice, 'Uncle Dan, my mummy and daddy aren't in their bed. Didn't they come home yet?'

Uncle Dan?

Cindy's eyes widened. She looked from him to the three children. The resemblance between all four was striking but, then. . .

Comprehension dawned and she suddenly felt very foolish. 'You're Andrew Sack's children,' she exclaimed.

Daniel raised his eyebrows at her for a moment. Then he grinned. 'You thought I was the father of all of these terrors?'

Cindy nodded abruptly.

Brittany put her hands on her hips. She scowled at Cindy aggressively.

Daniel intervened hastily. 'I have enough on my hands with one of them.' He gestured extravagantly at Susan and Will. 'Meet Susan and Will Sack, Dr James.'

His voice softened with pride and love as he turned to Brittany and gently tugged on a dark curl touching the frowning face. 'This beautiful one's mine.'

Brittany beamed at him but the scowl reappeared when she turned back to Cindy. 'He's *my* father.'

The friendly little girl of the day before was gone. Cindy was startled and a little hurt at the depth of animosity that glowered at her.

Daniel handed Will over to Brittany. 'Think you and Susan can change this young man for me, sweetheart? I've got to go back to the hospital in a moment, and I haven't finished talking to Cindy.'

Brittany heaved the small boy expertly onto one hip. She hesitated for a moment, then flung one last hostile look at Cindy, before walking out of the room.

Daniel knelt down and spoke gently to Susan. Cindy admired the way he explained that her father was having an operation to take away for good the bad pain that had been so scary. After a moment a much happier Susan raced out of the room.

'Daniel,' Cindy began hesitantly, 'I'm sorry I got it so wrong but they all look so much like you that it never even crossed my mind they weren't yours.'

'My sister and I are very alike. There's a strong mixture of Spanish and Italian blood in our ancestry on both sides.' He pulled a face. 'I'm the beautiful one, of course.'

Cindy's lips tilted. 'Of course,' she said smoothly, and his sudden grin of appreciation brought back the flood of feelings so strongly that she turned away to hide her face from him and started towards the door. If ever a man could be called beautiful this one certainly could!

Then she remembered and paused. Hesitantly she turned back and said softly, 'While we're sorting out these misunderstandings, you said something yesterday about your wife. . .' Her voice faltered and died at the spasm that crossed his face.

A mask slipped into place and she bitterly regretted her words as he said sharply, 'There's absolutely no need for us to discuss Sally. All you need to know is that she died three years ago. Brittany gets upset when anyone talks about her so I'd appreciate it if you never mentioned her mother in front of her. Now, about these keys and surgery times.'

Cindy numbly forced herself to listen to his hurried and brief explanations before he rushed away. It was obvious that mention of his wife's death was also still too painful for him as well as his daughter. Concern swept through her for the pair of them. Surely after three years they should have come to grips better than they had with losing someone they loved.

A frowning Casey delivered her clothes not long after she had helped Naomi get the children's breakfast and a still scowling Brittany ready for school. Cindy did her best to allay his concern for her, but she was glad Daniel was not there to have his opinion of her over-protective family confirmed.

'Well, at least promise me you won't try and unpack all that stuff at your flat by yourself, Cindy,' Casey growled at her at last.

Cindy gave a chuckle. 'No fear of that. Anyway, I'll

be sleeping here until Aileen comes home.' But definitely in another bedroom, she added to herself, and then felt remembered warmth flood her at the memories that brought and, yes, the sudden regret.

'Cindy?' Casey was looking at her with a strange look on his face.

That had always been the problem with having a twin who seemed to know what she was thinking!

The heat on her face deepened, but she smiled innocently and said quickly, 'Casey, I don't have time now to go myself, but there are a few things I could do with from the flat. Do you think you could find them and drop them around?'

Casey didn't say anything for a moment, just stared at her thoughtfully. Then, to her relief, he listened quietly to her hurried instructions, without asking the questions she knew he wanted to, and left a few moments later.

It was a rush, but Cindy was dressed in one of the neat skirts and tops she usually wore when working and was in the medical centre adjacent to the house, having a good look around, a few moments before a very attractive red-haired woman arrived.

The woman looked her up and down curiously but greeted her cheerfully enough. 'Hello, Dr James. I'm the receptionist, Jennifer Coats. I'm so pleased you're here at last.'

As the receptionist teetered on high-heeled red shoes behind the counter in the large, air-conditioned waiting room Cindy watched her thoughtfully. The woman was older than she had expected, and was dressed in a very smart, cream linen dress. The handbag she discarded exactly matched her red shoes. A little too dressy perhaps for a day in the medical centre of a small coastal town?

'Daniel rang me on his car phone this morning and told me what's happened. He said he hadn't mentioned that I'm a registered nurse as well and to tell you to give me plenty of work to do.'

Before Cindy could respond Jennifer smiled ruefully. 'Occasionally when they're terribly busy the docs get me to do some treatments as well as look after the front desk, especially when Aileen's here as well. They forget sometimes that when they're busy we are busier as well.'

Cindy stiffened slightly. There was something about this woman she did not like. She had met many different receptionists and knew this was a veiled request not to work her too hard.

She smiled politely and said sweetly, 'Men are like that, aren't they? I guess he told you I'm still officially on the sick list, but I will try and not make you do too much of my work.'

'Now,' she added briskly as Jennifer's smile faltered, 'what appointments do you have already? I would also appreciate you not making any more appointments for me today unless you check with me first.'

She didn't feel it necessary to tell her that she was afraid her strength would have worn out after the next few hours of getting through the long morning list she had already quickly perused.

'Anyone wanting a home visit you'd better put straight through for me to assess,' she added, hoping fervently there would not be any calls that could not be put off until Daniel returned. 'And now could you immediately let me have any charts for any patients who have been here before?'

The woman frowned slightly, but merely nodded a little abruptly.

Fortunately none of the patients were new ones. Cindy was able to glance quickly through the first few case histories before the first appointment, and breathed a soft sigh of relief when they looked like being reasonably straightforward.

Not having had a chance to familiarise herself with where equipment was stored, Cindy was much slower getting through the appointments than she would normally have been, and two hours later—after a postnatal check-up of a woman and her baby—she knew she was well behind. Despite knowing that the next patient had already been waiting far too long, she knew she had to take a well-deserved break.

After the young, beaming mother had left she finished writing up the notes on the new mother's chart, and then rested her head on her hands.

'Dr James, are you all right?'

Cindy raised her head and looked wearily at the receptionist.

'My goodness, you do look tired,' Jennifer exclaimed. 'You should have let me weigh that baby for you.'

After her comments earlier Cindy had felt ashamed of herself, and had refrained from asking for assistance from the obviously busy receptionist.

She managed a weak smile. 'Yes, I know. Any chance of a cup of tea before the next patient, Jennifer? And for heaven's sake call me Cindy when there are no patients around,' she said wearily, and propped her aching head on one hand again.

'You need an aspirin even more, by the look of you,' Jennifer said with a worried frown. 'You must have been really sick to tire so quickly. Are you sure you can cope with the rest?'

'I'll have to, won't I?' Cindy said grimly.

Jennifer hesitated, and said, 'Well, I can see if there are any of the patients who wouldn't mind postponing their appointments until Dr Burston can see them this evening or even later in the week, if you like.'

And why on earth didn't you do that earlier when

you were told there was only one doctor? Cindy thought grimly, and then knew that she should not have taken for granted that the woman would automatically do just that.

'Thank you,' she said crisply. 'I'd very much appreciate it. If seeing that handful of patients has already made me feel like this and anyone comes in who can't wait. . .' She shrugged.

Jennifer's face softened sympathetically. 'Right, I'll see what I can do. And I'll make your tea for you, too.'

After the short break Cindy found that a triumphant Jennifer had been able to make appointments for all except two, a woman with a feverish small child and an elderly man who had already been waiting for some time to see the doctor.

They were quickly dealt with, antibiotics and cough syrup for the child and renewal prescriptions for high blood pressure and anti-inflammatory medication for the frail old man who was accompanied by his daughter. Very thankfully, Cindy rather shakily made her escape at last back to the house.

She was grateful that Naomi refrained from commenting on her white face as she dished up the salad she had prepared for lunch. Cindy was almost too tired to eat, but forced some down so her sister would not worry any more than she was.

When Cindy at last pushed her plate away her sister said quietly, 'Daniel said we couldn't use Aileen's and Andrew's bedroom as she will, no doubt, be back and forwards from the hospital to check on the kids and get clean clothes and stuff, even probably stay overnight. So I've made up the fold-up bed in Will's and Susan's room for Brittany like he said to, Cindy. That leaves Brittany's bed in my room for you to go and rest on.

'Off you go. Right now,' she added very firmly, her

chin tilted ready to deal with any argument.

Cindy grimaced. 'You're horridly like your mother, young lady,' she grumbled.

Naomi merely grinned, although Cindy could see she was pleased at being compared to the mother they all grumbled about but loved dearly.

But, as weary as Cindy was when she did lie down, she could not sleep. Her brain was churning over the patients she had seen.

There was one particular young teenager she would have liked to ask Daniel about. Her mother had stayed in the room, despite Cindy tentatively suggesting she could wait outside. The young fifteen-year-old girl had been very thin and Cindy suspected she had an eating disorder, either anorexia or bulimia or both.

But the mother had been anxious and domineering, answering the questions for the young girl, so that the girl had hardly a chance to say anything. Cindy had ended up ordering some blood tests and asking them to make another appointment when the results would be back.

I should have been firmer with that woman, she thought wearily. Next time, there's no way I'll let her in with her daughter.

She must have dozed for a while because the next thing she knew was Naomi standing with an anxious face beside the bed, saying that Jennifer needed her at once back in the surgery.

The young man had jumped down a sand-hill and straight onto broken glass. When Cindy walked quickly up to the couch on which Jennifer had him lying, the large gash in the patient's foot was still bleeding quite profusely.

At all three of the other practices where Cindy had worked for her FMT she would have sent the young man, John Wills, straight to the emergency department at the nearest hospital just around the corner. But this surgery was well equipped to handle cases like this, with the nearest hospital well over an hour's travel away. So she grimly set to work to clean and repair the soft tissue damage, before at last thankfully putting in the long row of skin sutures.

After the long session Cindy gratefully left Jennifer to give him his tetanus injection boost, put a sterile dressing and support bandage over the sutured wound and fit him for a pair of crutches while she wrote up his notes. The sleep had refreshed her but she was dismayed to realise how quickly the wretched weakness had returned.

Cindy had just signed her name on the notes when the reception desk bell in the waiting room tinkled.

'Could you get that, Dr James?' Jennifer called loudly from the treatment room.

For a moment Cindy hesitated and then pushed herself upright. She stood still for a moment, fighting the wave of dizziness, and then slowly made her way out to the waiting room. She took one look at the white face and swaying figure of the woman holding a heavily blood stained teatowel around her hand and called urgently, 'Jennifer, come here.'

She started forward and unsuccessfully tried to grab the large woman as she started to crumple. The woman fell heavily to the floor.

Jennifer rushed in and helped her gently roll the woman over. She stared up at them from a very pale face and dazed eyes.

'The. . .axe. . . It slipped,' she gasped slowly.

Cindy quickly but very carefully unwrapped the teatowel. Blood was still dripping from the deep slash across the gaping wound on the back of the woman's hand.

A deep voice said calmly from the doorway to the

waiting room, 'Treating patients on the floor now, are we, girls?'

Cindy was so relieved to see him she couldn't even resent the 'girls' title. She stood up quickly, and the world started to spin horribly.

There was a sharp exclamation from Daniel and then Cindy felt strong arms come around her. For one moment she leaned thankfully against a warm, solid chest and felt safe and secure. Then he moved and lifted her up against him.

Cindy was so tall that no one had dared to carry her since she was a child, not even Casey when fooling around.

Just as well I've lost so much weight, she thought.

She realised she must have said it out loud when he grunted, 'Too much by the look of you.'

It felt good to be held so firmly. She could hear the steady thump of his heart, feel the play of his muscles. She caught her wayward thoughts firmly.

'I'm all right,' she muttered crossly. 'Look after that woman.'

'Jennifer's with her.'

The deep voice sounded angry again, and Cindy sighed. 'You're annoyed again.'

He was carefully putting her down on an examination couch, and she felt a pang go through her as he removed his arms.

'Stay there,' he said harshly, and disappeared.

'I don't think I've any choice,' Cindy murmured to the empty room and thankfully closed her eyes.

Several minutes later a fit of coughing forced her to sit up. It left her even more shaken and she looked helplessly at Daniel's grim face as he reappeared. Then she saw the wheelchair he was pushing.

'No.' Her voice was hoarse. 'I had enough of those in hospital.'

'I didn't know you had been hospitalised, but by the look of you perhaps you should still be in hospital.'

'No way!'

She glared at him, but relentlessly his arms came around her and then she was in the chair and being whisked out of the building and along the cement path to the house. She was very thankful there was no sign of Naomi or the children as he pushed her through the house into the bedroom she was to share with Naomi and then helped her onto the bed.

He surveyed her for a moment and abruptly strode from the room. She closed her eyes and brushed angrily at the weak tears forcing themselves between her eyelashes. Then she heard his firm stride and he appeared with a couple of pillows.

Gently he helped her sit up and placed the pillows behind her. He stood back and surveyed her. She held his gaze for a moment and then looked away.

The side of the bed sank down as he sat beside her. He reached for her hand and felt her pulse.

'Like I told you, I'm all right,' she muttered. 'Just a bit tired.'

'More than tired, I think. I'd say you are thoroughly exhausted.'

She didn't answer him. He was silent and at last she looked up at him. He was watching her carefully with a deep frown in his eyes.

'It was more than a chest infection and flu, wasn't it?'

She moistened her lips. 'Bronchopneumonia, resistant to the first course of antibiotics,' she said shortly.

His eyes darkened and she blurted out, 'Shouldn't you be looking after that patient?'

'I've tied off the bleeders and put in an IV line. The ambulance is on its way. She needs microsurgery in OT.' He paused, and the angry scowl which had again creased his face disappeared.

Cindy stared as tenderness transformed him. A gentle hand touched her face. 'I feel like an absolute heel. Why didn't you tell me you'd been so sick?'

She stiffened. 'Didn't Casey or Naomi tell you I wasn't supposed to start work for at least another week, and then only if my check-up was OK?'

He hesitated.

'Oh, yeah, that's right,' she said abruptly. 'You thought they were being too protective.'

'I'm very sorry, Cindy.' His voice was very deep and husky, filled with regret.

Cindy's eyes widened. In her experience, huge, dominant men like him and her three brothers and father very rarely apologised for anything.

'The only excuse I have is that this blonde, bikini-clad woman with unbelievably long legs and a gorgeous body appeared out of nowhere and rather threw me off balance.'

Mesmerised, Cindy stared into his eyes as he leaned closer. Heat flickered in their depths and she knew he was going to kiss her. At last. As she had longed for him to do ever since the heat of his appraisal in the office.

She closed her eyes and smelt the male fragrance of him, felt the softest, tentative touch of warm lips. He drew in a deep breath as though air was scarce. Strong arms grasped her shoulders, drew her closer still and then his lips had captured hers, bringing her whole body to a singing passionate response.

It can't happen as fast as this, she thought helplessly, it just can't.

'*Dad-dy!*'

The exclamation of absolute disgust ripped through the air.

Still in a daze, Cindy looked towards the doorway.

Brittany was staring at them with horror written all over her dirt-stained little face.

And this time there was no mistaking the dislike. No, it was more than that. This time there was fear and then sheer hatred towards the woman her father had dared to kiss.

CHAPTER FOUR

DANIEL muttered a short, sharp oath under his breath and withdrew from Cindy abruptly. His face grim, he stood up.

Naomi appeared behind Brittany and he barked out, 'Your sister's to stay in bed the rest of the day.' He swung his daughter up in his arms and disappeared.

Cindy stared at the empty doorway blankly, and then looked helplessly up at Naomi.

'Oh, Cindy, dear, I knew you shouldn't have worked so. . . Now, for goodness' sake, no tears!' As Naomi flew forward to give her a fierce hug Cindy closed her eyes, shutting out her sister's anxious face.

Swallowing back the tired, bewildered tears that had moistened her eyes, Cindy let Naomi fuss over her, and yielded weakly to her insistence to put on her nightdress so she could be 'more comfortable' and let her straighten the bedclothes as she slid at last back onto the bed.

Exhausted as she was, sleep did not come after Naomi had finished tucking her in and quietly pulled the door closed behind her. That passionate kiss had scorched her to her very soul, and when Daniel had wrenched his mouth from hers she had been left strangely unsatisfied, the kiss incomplete and her lips aching for more.

But what had it meant to him? The look on his face had held only bitter regret and anguish that his daughter had seen them.

Talk about bad timing! How could he have kissed her like that? No, that wasn't fair. She had been with him all the way. How could *they* have kissed like that, throwing caution to the wind? It had been almost inevitable that someone would have seen them.

Cindy frowned deeply. Why was Brittany being so antagonistic? It might be normal for a small girl who'd had her father to herself to feel jealous of any woman who came on the scene, but the depth of that hatred and fear had been far from normal.

A couple of hours later Cindy was tired of tossing and turning. She was grateful that Naomi had unpacked her suitcase. She found her dressing-gown but her hands faltered as she tied the sash, thinking of that other, well-washed and worn man's coat that had held the perfume of his spicy aftershave.

'Forget it, woman,' she admonished herself out loud. 'He's certainly already regretting kissing you and, remember, you have to work with him for the next six months.'

She finished hanging up the rest of her clothes in the built-in wardrobe, tidied the rest of her things neatly in the case and made her way rebelliously to the kitchen.

Naomi was pouring pasta into a steaming saucepan and scowled at her. 'What are you doing up? Daniel said you were to stay there until morning.'

'I'm sick to death of bed.'

'Oh, yeah? What about if you have company in the said bed?'

Cindy gaped at her, her pulse doing all kinds of strange things.

Naomi grinned far too innocently back at her. 'I'm sure you'd enjoy a nice young man in your bed.'

'Now, now, I mean young Will,' she added hastily as Cindy opened her mouth angrily. 'He gives great big sloppy kisses, too.'

'Naomi. . .' Cindy began tersely and then stopped, not quite sure how to put into words that teasing about that kiss was definitely not appreciated without giving it more importance than was wise.

Before she found the words Naomi added hastily, 'Sorry, big sis. Brittany told me what she interrupted.' She frowned suddenly at Cindy. 'She was *very* upset with you kissing her precious father, Cindy.'

'Yes, I know.'

Naomi studied her for a moment. 'He didn't seem too upset, though,' she muttered at last.

'Oh, for goodness' sake! He was only being sorry I'd had to work so hard!'

And that's *all* it was. At least on his part, she tried to convince herself. A tinge of regret stroked through Cindy. Her lips still felt bereft, and she only realised her hand was rubbing them when she suddenly saw Naomi's eyes following the movement.

She knew she was starting to blush and was thankful for her sister's sensitivity when she only smiled gently and said breezily, 'If you like, you can have young Will join you on the bed as long as you can put up with his wriggles. Just chase him out if he becomes too much. It would be a huge help to have him out of my hair while I finish getting tea ready.'

'Where are the other two kids?'

'Just getting dressed after their baths. Now, you, back to bed before Daniel catches you! He was really upset that you nearly fainted.'

'I didn't faint!'

'Well, not far off it from what he said. Now I'll ring Casey,' she threatened. 'In fact, I'll even ring Mum and tell her to come here to look after you if you so much as dare appear in this kitchen until morning,' Naomi flashed at her.

Cindy stared at her sister's determined face and subsided with, 'I feel sorry for any poor kids you ever have. I think you'll be worse than Mum's ever been.'

Then she grinned a little crookedly at the pleased expression that filled her sister's face at the compliment. She turned to obey her, and then remembered.

'Have you heard if Andrew had his operation today and how he is?'

'Daniel said he is minus one gall bladder, but. . .' Naomi glanced cautiously around to make sure none of the children had come in '. . .there are a few complications and risk of infection so they think he'll be there quite a while.'

Cindy frowned. She could only guess at the complications but, no doubt, pancreatitis could be one. 'I hope you don't mind staying, Naomi,' she said slowly.

Naomi flashed her a grin. 'Piece of cake, especially with the beach so close.'

Despite her protests, Cindy had to confess the next morning that the enforced stay in bed had certainly made her feel much better. Will had gleefully brought her a pile of books and toys to play with until teatime. Later, Susan had shyly presented herself with her favourite book to be read out loud, and Cindy had enjoyed herself immensely.

The only drawback had been the inner tension as she waited for Daniel to appear, wondering just how she should behave towards him. But although Cindy had heard Brittany's and her father's voices in the house neither had come near her.

Not even to say goodnight, she had thought sadly as she had at last given up and turned off her light to fall into a deep sleep.

The next morning she dressed carefully in one of her cool, professional-looking navy and white cotton dresses she usually wore to work. She was starting on her second cup of tea before Daniel put in an appearance in the kitchen.

'What do you think you're doing?'

He had an angry, taut look. Cindy felt warmth touch her own face but forced herself to say calmly, 'Having some breakfast. A cup of tea for you?'

She went to rise, and he moved quickly and waved her away. 'I can wait on myself,' he snapped, 'and you're supposed to be still resting.'

Cindy picked up her cup and took a long, refreshing sip. It gave her a chance to settle the nerves that had started jumping all over the place as her eyes settled for a moment on those lips that had brought hers to life.

'No, I've had my rest.' Her voice was steady and she returned his glare with full measure. 'I'm helping you with surgery this morning.' Whether you like it or not, her defiant look added.

His scowl deepened. 'Your health is more important. I'm doing surgery this morning.'

'Jennifer told me yesterday that usually both doctors take surgery Tuesday mornings. And she changed a few appointments from yesterday so the list is even longer.'

The anger on his face deepened, and as he went to interrupt her she added quickly, 'I'm not stupid enough to try and work as long as I did yesterday. You might say the extent of my weakness surprised me more than you.'

Suddenly the scowl was gone from his face. He stared at her for a moment and then he smiled, and that teasing light that so transformed him made her draw in a quick, shallow breath and quickly put down her cup.

It just wasn't fair. He shouldn't be so devastating. How could she remain firm with the resolve that had made her set her alarm, shower, dress and be ready to defeat all arguments?

'It certainly surprised me,' he said softly.

By the gleam in his eyes she was suddenly sure he was referring to more than her exhaustion. So he thought that allowing him to kiss her had been a weakness, did he?

She had gone over and over that heavenly kiss, and had come to the conclusion that, wonderful as it had been, it had definitely been a bad mistake.

Trying to convince herself that she never wanted it repeated was a little harder.

He was her boss.

She had to survive working with him for six months.

She had her final requirements for becoming a GP to work towards and didn't need any distractions, especially from one of her supervisors.

She wanted to be friends with that likeable little daughter of his with whom she had been getting on so well, not make an enemy of her.

So kisses were out.

She didn't need his kisses.

And she knew she was lying desperately to herself.

Daniel was studying her hot cheeks with interest. She refused to look away. Her chin went up another notch.

'I won't work myself into that state again,' she said steadily, 'and each day I'm a little stronger. This time you'll be around to take over if I get too tired.'

'I don't believe you.'

'I beg your pardon!'

'You're so dedicated to your career you'll forfeit your own well-being for it.' His voice was flat, all amusement gone. Instead, there was a flash of angry derision in his face.

'And what doctor worth his salt would not put his own welfare second to his patients'?'

'Any doctor worth anything at all would know that without reasonable care of her own body, soul and spirit she can only cause harm to patients, no matter how well meaning she is. Exhaustion can affect your judgement.'

'I agree wholeheartedly, but you should tell that to the

powers that be in hospitals that expect too much of young graduates.'

'I have,' he snorted. 'During the last three years I've even written articles for medical journals about it. Almost everyone agrees with me, but the reality is. . .'

He paused, and after a long moment she finished softly for him, 'The reality is that there's never enough money to hire enough medical personnel and we can't see a patient suffer, even die, if we can do anything to prevent it.'

There was a shadow in his eyes but he said sharply, 'Well, that's not the case in this practice. And I'm not talking about life and death situations—I'm talking about the driving ambition that some doctors have to gain knowledge and experience to advance their career. I'm talking about stupid, pig headed—'

He stopped abruptly and turned away. Cindy watched his rigid back for a moment. There was more here than he was telling her. Some bad experience in the past? Surely not his own father! Dr Burston senior had very obviously impressed her as a doctor who cared very deeply for his patients, but he had spoken of his wife and children with great affection.

There was no chance to ask any of the questions that filled her mind. Naomi appeared, yawning mightily, followed by Brittany. They both stopped when they saw Cindy. The little girl frowned and stared silently from her father to Cindy. Naomi put her hands on her hips.

Before she could speak Cindy rose decisively. 'I'm going across to the surgery in a few minutes. I didn't have a chance yesterday to familiarise myself with the layout as much as I'd have liked to.' With an effort she had succeeded in keeping her voice very firm, and added abruptly as Naomi opened her mouth, 'And Daniel has said all there is to say.'

Naomi rolled her eyes at her and looked at Daniel.

She ignored them both and strode towards the door.

Daniel's voice said quietly, 'She'll be all right. I'll keep a very close eye on her today.'

Cindy turned in time to see some unspoken communication between Naomi and Daniel, and decided that immediate retreat was strategic. She had only taken one more step towards the door when there was the patter of little feet and Will trotted into the room. Susan was close behind him.

Then Cindy remembered with shame that she had hardly given a thought to Andrew Sack. She swung back and asked guiltily, 'Have you heard from Aileen? Is Andrew doing OK?'

Will had made a beeline for Daniel and, his face transformed by love, his uncle was swinging the small boy up into his arms. Will squealed with delight and Daniel gave a deep chuckle.

Cindy felt her heart squeezed. If he felt like this about his nephew, how much more would he love his own son? And there was no doubting the love he had for his daughter.

'He's doing fine.' The child's voice was unnaturally loud. Cindy blinked and tore her eyes away from Daniel's laughing face. Brittany was sullenly watching her.

'Auntie Aileen said she'll be home later today.' As the small, tense figure continued the words were polite enough, but Cindy heard the underlying hostility. 'So you won't have to stay here any longer.'

'Don't be too sure of that. I have the feeling that your aunt will simply check up on her terrors but be back and forth to the hospital.' Daniel tossed Will up into the air again. 'Knowing my sister, she won't be able to keep away from Andrew's side for long, and she won't want this bundle of dynamite terrorising the other patients and hospital staff. So our arrangement stays for a bit longer, if it's all right with you both.'

Daniel hesitated, looked steadily at Cindy and added softly, 'Probably quite a bit longer, I'm afraid. There were problems.' He glanced swiftly at the listening Brittany, before adding, 'Just a bit of pancreatitis as well.'

Cindy knew he was playing down Andrew's condition for the children's sake, but her heart sank. Andrew could be in hospital for a couple of weeks and would probably have a much longer convalescence.

To Cindy's relief, Naomi smiled at Daniel. 'As long as I can go to the beach whenever I can and get home in plenty of time to do some Christmas shopping,' she said cheerfully.

Daniel's face lightened. He smiled back at her. 'Seeing that Christmas is a good six weeks away still, I'd say that will be no problem at all.'

He swung Will to the floor and the bundle of dynamite promptly laughed up at his uncle and toddled straight for the table. It was Naomi who grabbed him just before he succeeded in pulling the tablecloth and everything sitting on it onto the floor.

'Will, behave! Come on, kids,' Naomi said firmly. 'Sit up and have your breakfast. Brittany, you're going to be late for school if you don't get a move on.'

Cindy stared with considerable respect at her baby sister as all the children proceeded to do as they had been told. She had, indeed, sounded just like their own mother scolding her brood into action.

She glanced up and saw Daniel's smothered grin. He caught her looking at him and his face relaxed into a wide smile.

'She's a natural,' he murmured. 'Come on, let's go while the going's good.'

She hesitated. 'It's pretty early for you to come. I just wanted to familiarise myself more with the place.'

'No problem,' he said crisply. 'I'll show you over as I should have yesterday.'

'By the way,' Daniel said as he unlocked the surgery a few moments later, 'I managed to get a message to Mum and Dad about Andrew late last night. They were still in Canberra.'

'So, what are you going to do with only half a doctor to help?' Cindy asked, attempting a smile. 'Will you be able to get a locum at short notice?'

'It's very doubtful at this time of the year.' He turned and looked seriously back at Cindy. 'Besides, from what happened yesterday, you were quite a bit more than half a doctor.'

She pulled a face. 'But I was certainly finished for the day. What if there had been more emergencies?'

'Then they would have had to wait for the ambulance like anyone does in areas without a local doctor.'

He had stood back and gestured to Cindy to enter the office, and she heard him add in a mutter, No matter how Dad would hate it.'

As he moved in behind her he said in a slightly mocking voice, 'Oh, and Dr James, you'll be pleased to hear that your very first patient, Baby Owens, was discharged yesterday from hospital with a clean bill of health.'

Cindy felt a flush heat her cheeks. 'Er, that's very good,' she said quickly. 'Let's hope the parents have a bit more sense in the future.'

'They certainly should after the word I had with them.' Daniel's voice was stern and Cindy was glad she had not been on the end of his displeasure.

Fortunately the word must have spread in the small community that one of the regular doctors was in hospital himself and there were no new appointments, except another of the early holiday-makers from one of the local motels.

Jennifer was again very well dressed, and far more efficient than Cindy had first supposed. But for some reason Cindy found that easy, friendly relationship with Daniel irritated her a few times.

Daniel was adamant that Cindy only stay for a couple of hours, and she knew he must have made sure she saw only routine, minor cases. Even so, she refused to admit to him how tired she was when he told her brusquely to go home.

How right he was in knowing his father hated seeing the people in this small town without sufficient medical help was verified late that afternoon. Cindy was woken from another enforced afternoon rest by the sound of a booming voice in the house.

She was still for a moment, and then grinned with relief. Dr Burston senior was home. She had liked the elderly man very much. It was obvious that he was a very dedicated and caring doctor from the disappointed faces of most of his patients that she had seen that morning.

Bounding off the bed, she quickly tidied herself, took a deep breath and headed towards the office and the sound of two male voices.

'Stupid woman,' Dr Burston senior was growling when Cindy hastily entered the office.

She paused, her heart sinking, but he looked up at her and his scowl lifted. 'Not you, girl, that stupid mother of Dan's!'

'Please note that she's my mother when he's had a row with her, not his wife!'

Cindy looked across the room at Daniel, sprawled in the large chair behind the desk. He smiled at her, but she saw that it did not reach his eyes.

'And she's not at all stupid. I agree with her entirely.' Daniel stood up. 'I've just been telling Dad there was no need for him to fly home from Canberra. We can cope, can't we, Cindy?'

He stared at her commandingly and she rushed in to

say cheerfully,' Goodness, yes! I'm just so very sorry I couldn't come when I was booked to, Dr Burston, but I'm sure I'll be a different woman in another few days.'

'Are you sure about that, young lady? Jim Clarke informed me it was a pretty nasty bout of staph aureus pneumonia you copped.'

'You didn't tell me Cindy had pneumonia, Dad.'

Why, he sounded really annoyed with his father!

Cindy looked from one man to the other. Surprisingly, Daniel's father was not at all like his son in general appearance. He was much shorter, and if his hair had ever been black it was now snowy white.

'Too many other things to worry about,' the elderly man was saying tersely. 'The way your mother was carrying on at the time you'd have thought we never went on holidays.'

'You didn't. Your patients always took first place.' Daniel's voice was sharp. He turned away quickly and said in a slightly milder voice, 'And there was really no need for you to cut short your trip this time either.'

'Your father actually agreed with you, but when our only son-in-law is rushed to hospital and undergoes surgery I'd say there was every need, son,' a resigned voice said from behind Cindy. 'But I'm sure there's no reason for him to stay and work!'

Cindy swung around and saw a tall, stately woman standing in the doorway, and knew she had been right. Daniel was more like his mother than his father. Brittany was clinging to her grandmother's hand with a beaming look on her face. It changed to a very watchful expression as soon as she saw Cindy.

Mrs Burston strode forward and held out her hand to Cindy. 'Hello, you must be Dr James,' she said briskly. 'I'm sorry Aileen and I were away the day you had your interview, and I'm sorry you've been landed in this mess.'

'She fainted yesterday.' Brittany stared accusingly up at Cindy for a moment and then walked across to her grandfather and said in a very grown-up voice, 'I don't think she's the right person for this practice, Grandad. I heard Jennifer tell Dad so. She told Mrs Campbell, too.'

Cindy stared at the small girl and then her eyes met Daniel's. He looked uncomfortable for a moment, and her eyes narrowed. Had he been discussing her with their receptionist?

'Brittany, that's very rude,' Daniel said sharply. 'And you're wrong, and so is Jennifer,' he added, his eyes capturing Cindy's for a long moment. 'Perhaps in the beginning I did have some doubts, but the way she has shown dedication to our patients at the risk of her own health shows she is a very good doctor.'

For some reason his words did not sound like a compliment at all, but after a moment of disquiet Cindy murmured, 'Thank you, Daniel.' Then she turned back to his mother.

'I'm so sorry your holiday has been interrupted, Mrs Burston, but as soon as you've seen that Andrew is getting on all right there's no need for you not to resume it, is there?'

'None at all,' Daniel agreed, his voice emphatic. 'In fact, Naomi and Cindy can continue our arrangement so Mum doesn't get too tired looking after the kids.'

His father raised his head, but Daniel added forcefully, 'Cindy and I will be able to manage for the next few weeks until Andrew's on his feet again. If we get inundated some patients will just have to make the trip to the city.'

Dr Burston senior scowled and opened his mouth, but his wife said quickly, 'Just as they had to before you ever started the practice and initiated the ambulance setting up a base here! Oh, I know the town was half its present size but they didn't even have one ambulance in those early days for this whole area. Now, you promised to take the children to the hospital as soon as you'd had a word with Daniel.'

Her husband frowned and looked doubtfully from Cindy to Daniel. 'But what about the evening surgery and the house calls? You're still as white as a ghost, girl, and Jennifer said she'd had to talk quite a few patients into other appointments.'

Daniel's lips tightened. 'She's exaggerating.'

Anger had deepened his voice and Cindy felt a fleeting wave of sympathy for the receptionist.

'Cindy managed very well this morning and is going to do the evening surgery while I do the calls.'

'Of course I am.' Cindy backed him up quickly. 'Yesterday I did overdo it a bit, but I managed very well this morning.'

She raised her head and avoided looking at Daniel, who had earlier curtly told her she was not to go near the surgery until the next morning.

Dr Burston looked from one to the other, and then he said reluctantly, 'Well, if you're sure. . .?'

'Of course they'll manage without your help,' Mrs Burston said crossly. 'They obviously have so far, and Daniel told you on the phone they were getting on very well together.'

Cindy felt pleased but reminded herself he would have said so even if it wasn't true. But the fact was that they had worked together very well those couple of hours.

'Dad likes her so much he kissed her this morning.'

All the adults stared down at Brittany. Her voice had been filled with disgust.

Cindy knew her face was crimson. She glanced quickly at Daniel. He was looking at his mother with the strangest expression. Mrs Burston was staring back at him and Cindy could not tell from her expression whether she approved or not.

Dr Burston gave what sounded like a sniffled chortle. 'Did he just? I'd say you are right, then, Brittany, although I don't think your father usually kisses everyone he likes, especially not someone he only met yesterday. Perhaps only the pretty ones?'

'Really! No matter how much liking or how pretty, you are both *doctors*! And in front of your daughter.'

Cindy stared at Mrs Burston and her heart sank. Her face was full of censure.

Daniel was scowling back at her. 'Leave it, Mother.'

Cindy raised her chin and stared back at them all calmly. There was no way she would apologise or feel regret for that kiss she had enjoyed so much. Brittany looked very pleased with herself as she looked up at her grandmother.

So did her grandfather.

Cindy's lips suddenly twitched at the look of obvious approval and respect he was giving his son. But then Cindy looked at Mrs Burston and all desire to smile vanished.

Her eyes were narrowed as she stared at Cindy. She was frowning, and there was no mistaking the disapproval and dislike on her face.

Great. Here she was, seriously attracted, falling fast for this dynamic, handsome man, and already she had managed to alienate probably the two most important women in his life—his mother and his daughter!

CHAPTER FIVE

DANIEL'S mother and father stayed at their nearby house. Cindy had already found out that Daniel and Brittany had actually been sharing his parents' large house since they had moved to Sandy Cove. That first day she had arrived he had decided it was best not to disrupt the already upset children any more than necessary by letting them stay in their familiar surroundings.

The morning after the Burstons' return Cindy was again having breakfast by the time Daniel arrived in the kitchen.

'Good morning,' he said crisply in response to her murmured greeting. 'Thank you for coming over to the surgery last night.'

Cindy scowled at him. 'Not that you let me do a thing except sit and listen.'

He grinned at her. 'I'm sure you learnt a lot, Dr James.'

Because Cindy had still been feeling very weary by last night, she reluctantly smiled back. 'Not a thing I didn't already know, Dr Burston. Except,' she added after swallowing the last of her coffee, 'that some parents on holidays don't like missing a day at the beach for such a mundane thing as visiting the doctor with a sick child.'

Daniel scowled. 'Selfish beggars! I've heard Dad complain of that often over the years. Evening surgery is supposed to be for more urgent cases than a child who has been complaining of earache all day.'

'Oh, well, sometimes kids don't complain enough either when the sand and sun are waiting to be enjoyed.' Cindy hesitated, and said slowly, 'Daniel, it was obvious that you don't want your father to work while he's here, but are we going to be able to handle everything—house visits as well—if it gets as busy as Monday was?'

'Cindy, Dad's had very high blood pressure which he's been trying to control with medication for some time. He started having angina attacks several weeks back,' Daniel said abruptly. 'He had to stop work. That's why I pushed through the sale of my practice in Sydney and came earlier than we had planned. There's no way Mum and I want him to be worried again about this place before he's had a decent holiday. If necessary, some people can go to the hospital outpatient service, as Mum said.'

'Don't you think that will worry him more?'

'Not if we don't tell him.'

Cindy stood up. 'Well, I'm sure I can do a couple of the house calls for you today.'

'No way.'

'Now, look here, Daniel, as long as I'm not on my feet too long or work too many hours straight—'

She stopped abruptly as Daniel pushed back his chair and stood up. He was scowling again, and suddenly she didn't want to be the cause of his frown when his gorgeous smile did such devastating things to her nervous system.

'If I won't let Dad work because he's not well enough there's no way I'd let you either, Cindy James, so don't argue.'

Cindy drew a deep breath. 'Then I'll just have to prove to you that I am well, won't I?' she snapped.

'As soon as you do that we'll be sharing the work as evenly as possible.'

Cindy glared at him suspiciously for a moment, before turning and marching out. She didn't trust that 'as possible' one bit. It was obvious that he was as determined to mollycoddle her as she was to prove she could cope.

And she did cope well over the next couple of days.

Dr Burston poked his nose in a few times but they both were able to reassure him that he was not needed. Fortunately the workload was not too onerous, but Friday was a different matter. Too many people had decided that a visit to the doctor was imperative before the surgery was closed, except for emergencies, for the weekend. On Thursday Daniel had looked at the appointment book for the next day and growled at the number Jennifer had squeezed in.

'I'm sorry, Dr Burston.' The receptionist had given a little nervous laugh. 'I had to re-book quite a few from Monday and Tuesday, and others were very insistent. . .'

'It's all right, Jennifer,' Cindy said quickly. 'I'm quite a bit stronger now.' Which was true but, to her absolute disgust, she still tired far too quickly, something she had made every effort to keep Daniel from realising.

'We'll do surgery together, and then you can come with me later to call on some patients at home,' he had said decisively, and added to the receptionist, 'Ring those on the home visit list and tell them not to expect us until the afternoon.'

She had refrained from arguing in front of Jennifer and, in truth, was rather relieved and also pleased that he was at last letting her do home calls.

But in that she was mistaken.

'You mean, I'm not actually doing any house calls, just keeping you company?' she said angrily after a belated lunch when he had bundled her out to his gleaming black car.

'No, that's not what I mean at all,' Daniel said a little too smoothly. 'I have at least two houses I can drop you off at while I do other calls nearby. You won't tire yourself out driving, and I won't have to spend for ever re-dressing Mrs Hoad's ulcers.'

By the time Cindy had attended to the massive ulcers on both of the loquacious Mrs Hoad's legs, she knew that he really had needed her to do them to save his time.

Unfortunately the area was not serviced by home nursing, and so the doctors had to do several jobs that a trained nurse could have done. Mrs Hoad's varicose ulcers was one of them.

Daniel quickly filled Cindy in as he drove up the long, rough driveway to the old lady's ramshackle cottage. He told her the technical details of the treatment he had initiated for Mrs Hoad and then added, 'She's one very independent old lady. Apparently, she had been treating herself by wrapping bits of rag around her legs over some revolting old ointment she must have had for dozens of years.

'Goodness knows how long she put off all enquiries from concerned relatives and friends about them before the day they became so infected that her daughter noticed she had a fever and hauled her off to see me. Unfortunately, the daughter lives too far away to see her often, and Mrs Hoad refused point-blank to go to hospital or to let anyone else bring her to the surgery three times a week for the ulcers to be dressed.'

The thin, upright old lady glared at Cindy suspiciously as Daniel introduced her briefly, before hurrying back to his car.

Mrs Hoad turned abruptly and, leaning heavily on her walker, led the way to a spotlessly clean but very shabby kitchen. 'That Jenny Coats was right. You are a pretty thing, although not as short as she said.'

'You know our receptionist, Mrs Hoad?'

The old lady eased herself into an old lounge chair. She snorted. 'Known that Jenny since she came to live here with that no-good husband of hers. They used to manage a local fruit shop. She's been much better off since he up and off, especially since she started working for the doc. Used to be a nurse, she says. She right about you living with the young doc? I don't know what you young people think you're coming to. Morals gone out the window!'

Cindy caught her breath. Very carefully she placed her bag on the kitchen table. 'My sister and I are staying at Dr Sack's place while he is in hospital to help with the children,' she said mildly, feeling anything but. 'Did Jennifer really tell you Dr Burston and I are. . .are. . .?'

Mrs Hoad looked up from unwinding the thick elastic bandage that covered her leg from toes to knee. She studied Cindy for a moment, and suddenly grinned wickedly. 'Oh, it weren't me she was talkin' to. Too uppity for me these days she is. No, it was the postman. Said she was very coy about it, but gave him the wink, or so he said.'

Small-town gossip. That's all it was, Cindy tried to convince herself, but she did not like the idea of Jennifer talking about them at all. She was tempted to tell Daniel about it, but by the time he picked her up she had decided it would be too embarrassing. The nasty, large ulcer had been re-dressed with the special cream with which Daniel was treating it, and she had consumed two leisurely cups of tea before she heard his car return.

'That visit took you long enough,' she said with feeling as they waved goodbye to Mrs Hoad. 'We'll be very late by the time we finish the rest if they all take this long.'

'No, we won't,' Daniel said cheerfully. 'I've just done two. That's why I was so long. They were both calls on elderly folk, living by themselves. They suffer from multiple health problems, and with no public transport or a taxi service it's very difficult for them to get to the medical centre regularly. One of them, a Mrs Blackie, has her daughter from Sydney staying with her for a few weeks so that's one we can cross off our list until she goes home. Apparently, she's been trying to persuade her mother to go and live with her.

'She's a real old tartar but the way she has deteriorated,

even in the short time I've been seeing her, I hope the daughter succeeds,' he said, and then added sadly, 'Although she's such an independent old dear I don't know how she'll cope, with Ellen fussing over her all the time.'

Cindy glanced at him warmly. She liked the way he cared about each and every one of his patients. That had been very obvious from many things she had overheard him say at the surgery and when filling her in on the case histories of those on his house list today.

The last two patients were on the other side of Sandy Cove, a little distance out of town. Cindy accompanied Daniel into each house, where he introduced her with the excuse that he was showing the town's newest doctor the area and where the patients lived that she would soon be visiting by herself.

The first one was another of the town's elderly citizens. Once again Cindy was scrutinised very carefully by the stooped-over old man before he gave her an approving grin and winked at Daniel.

The last call was to a young woman in the last weeks of her pregnancy who had to be checked for high blood pressure. Daniel explained that her husband had been out of work for some time and been forced to take a temporary job some distance away so she had no help with the children during the week They were trying to get her to rest as much as possible, and visiting her at home instead of her having to drag herself and her two children to the surgery had helped.

The moment the two small children saw Daniel they made a rush for him.

Cindy smiled gently as she watched him tease them, before at last letting them rummage in his pockets until they found a small packet of jelly beans.

As she eased herself onto a chair beside a table the pale-faced woman protested wearily, 'You shouldn't spoil them every time you come, Doctor. It's good enough of you to put me on your house call list.'

Daniel let Cindy take Mrs Threadgate's blood pressure and test the sample of urine she had ready for them while he played with the children. The answers to their other questions and examinations were as satisfactory as the tests, and Daniel beamed at the young, obviously worried woman.

'Good girl, Joan,' he said warmly. 'Blood pressure's right down at last and everything else seems fine.'

Tears of relief filled the woman's face as she smiled back at him. 'And that's thanks to you, Dr Burston. That woman you organised from your church to come and help me has been great. Don and I are so grateful for all you've done for us.'

Daniel looked slightly embarrassed and brushed it off with a grin, before quickly saying goodbye and then pretending to race the squealing children out to the car. Cindy said her own goodbyes, noting how much younger Joan Threadgate seemed with the anxious look gone from her face.

As they drove off she settled back in her seat with a contented sigh. Even in the other three practices there had not been this same level of caring for the patients. The first two had been very big, very busy practices in large cities and the last one in Sydney, of course, had been the last straw. She decided then and there that if she ever bought into a practice it would have to be a small, family practice like this one.

Would Daniel and Andrew need another partner in the near future? she found herself wondering wistfully. Perhaps if she made herself irreplaceable during these next six months. . .

'So, how do you like Sandy Cove so far, Dr James?' Daniel asked suddenly.

'I like it very much, Dr Burston,' Cindy replied

enthusiastically with a delighted laugh. Anyone would think he was a mind-reader!

They had driven several kilometres out of Sandy Cove. The houses they had visited had been on small acreages, probably once part of small farms, Daniel had told Cindy comfortably.

'It's lovely here,' Cindy said as they came over the crest of a hill and saw the blue ocean stretching away to the horizon. 'You were very fortunate to grow up in such a beautiful place.'

Daniel was silent for so long that she turned and studied his strong profile. For some reason he looked a little grim. Then he glanced at her. There was a shadow in his dark eyes.

'Yes, I guess we were,' he said slowly. 'Trouble was, we didn't really appreciate it at all. Dad was usually far too busy to take us anywhere, although Mum did her best. It was sometimes too peaceful—except in the summer holidays, of course,' he added with a slight smile. 'I couldn't wait to get away to the city when I was a teenager, and when I'd been away at university for a couple of years all I wanted to do was come back to the sun and surf.'

'Well, I'd much rather live here than where I've been working for the last six months in inner Sydney,' Cindy said with a slight shudder.

He glanced at her again. There was speculation and curiosity in his glance this time. 'I know you came from a practice in Sydney to us but where did you do your other two lots of six months, and how come you heard about us? Dad said he hadn't even had a chance to advertise that he needed someone when you wrote to him.'

'My sister-in-law, Kim—Casey's wife—is one of Dr Burston's patients. Apparently, she knows Aileen fairly well and she mentioned it to her. Casey rang me straight away.'

'Casey's your twin, isn't he? What other family do you have, Cindy, and where do they live?'

Cindy smiled gently as she thought of her close-knit, loving family. 'I have two older brothers besides Casey. Mum and Dad still live on the dairy farm in the Hunter Valley where the five of us grew up. We all spoil Naomi rotten because she wasn't born until Casey and I were almost twelve.'

'Well, the way she's been helping out has really impressed my family so I don't think your spoiling has done her any harm.'

'She's very much like our mother, much more than I am,' Cindy said a little wistfully.

Daniel studied her for a moment. It was a penetrating gaze, and she looked away and said hurriedly, 'Dad's been a wonderful father, but we all adore Mum. Even now that we've grown up nothing seems to delight her more than when we get a bit sick so she can lavish all her love on us. We tease her mercilessly about being a frustrated nurse, but we all put up with her ministrations as graciously and for as long as each of our natures can—and love her dearly.'

'And yet you opted for a career ahead of a family of your own.'

Daniel's voice had been a little terse and she opened her mouth to refute that, but he suddenly looked across at her again and this time there was such a depth of sadness on his face that she swallowed and couldn't speak.

She had been going to tell him that they also teased her mother that her caring nature had manifested itself in all her children which was especially why, according to their brothers and sister, Cindy and her older brother, Benjamin, had chosen the medical profession as careers, but that she herself longed for a husband and children of her own to love.

'I wish Sally had grown up in a family more like yours,' Daniel murmured. 'Perhaps then she would have known what Brittany was missing out on.'

Cindy looked at him sharply. It was the first time he had mentioned his wife since that first disastrous day. She opened her mouth to ask him about her, but he was slowing the car to swing into the driveway back at the house and Brittany came racing out to glare at Cindy and be swept up in a hug from her father.

Fortunately, the weekend was fairly quiet, with only a handful of patients ringing up out of hours for various relatively minor emergencies. Daniel bluntly refused all offers of help from both Cindy and his father.

On Sunday morning everyone except Daniel went to the surprisingly large local church. When he was called out to a patient just as they were all ready to leave Cindy was astonished at how disappointed she suddenly felt.

After a delicious lunch, for which Mrs Burston had insisted on being responsible, Cindy was glad to be able to help Naomi play quietly with Will and Susan while their grandparents took Brittany in for her turn to visit her uncle. Aileen had been home to stay the night before and to do some washing for herself and Andrew. It was a very upset little girl and boy who waved their mother off, and it took all their ingenuity to distract the pair.

At last the tots were persuaded to have a Sunday nap. Just as Daniel returned from the medical centre Naomi stated firmly that she was going to lie down with a block of chocolate and enjoy the romantic novel she had bought the day before.

Daniel sank onto the lounge chair across from Cindy. 'The kids asleep?'

Cindy nodded. 'Yes, thank goodness. They were pretty upset they couldn't go to see their father.'

'The couple of times during the week they went in

with Mum and Dad was enough for Andrew,' Daniel said a little grimly. 'Apparently, they did nothing but fight and argue about who would sit next to him on the bed, and then Will was quickly bored and was a little terror to staff and other patients alike. Mum said he wore her out.'

Cindy laughed. 'He's gorgeous, but he is a human dynamo when he gets going.'

Daniel closed his eyes and relaxed with a sigh. She watched him silently for a while. She had been going to ask him if they would be having regular sessions at the surgery to review patients but hesitated to disturb one of the rare moments this last week when he had relaxed.

During her first six months of her FMT her supervisor had insisted for the first few weeks on daily sessions together, and only then weekly. For the last six months she had only met with her supervisor every month or when she herself initiated it.

She smiled as she watched Daniel for a long moment. He was so organised that she knew he would mention it when he was ready. So, instead, she, too, abandoned any idea of writing her regular letter home to her parents and closed her own eyes before she was tempted beyond endurance to go over, plonk herself on his lap and ask for another one of those kisses he had given her that very first morning in his bedroom.

Was it possible that was only a week ago? Living together in the same house meant that you got to know someone so much faster than otherwise.

But I wouldn't mind getting to know more about his kisses, she found herself thinking wistfully, then frowned and forced herself to think of something else.

She had almost dozed off at last when Daniel stirred and said, 'Phew, it's hot today. Anyone would think it was mid-summer instead of almost the end of spring.'

As Cindy opened her eyes he stood up, stretched

and wiped sweat from his face with a handkerchief.

'Feel like a swim at the beach?'

She had been staring at the way his jeans moulded and clung to his lean hips, and she tore her gaze away from the delicious sight to look at his face and say a little breathlessly, 'It would be lovely, but I'm not sure. . .'

'Aw, come on, Cindy. I haven't been near the beach for weeks, and it's not as much fun by myself,' he coaxed.

Cindy had been going to say she didn't think her energy would last as long as she would like it to for swimming, but she stood up and said gaily, 'Right, we can't have Dr Burston missing out on any fun when he's been working so hard.'

His eyes gleamed at her, and those well-shaped lips tilted in the smile she suddenly realised she often looked for.

'Be ready in five minutes? And, Cindy,' he called softly as she stood up and made for the door, 'I hope you've still got that red bikini.'

The trouble was, she realised furiously as she hurriedly changed, it was still the only swimming costume she had with her! All week she had been hoping to get a chance to unpack some of her things at the flat, but she had decided it would be wiser to conserve her energy for work.

Naomi raised her head from the paperback in her hand and blinked at her with a dazed look when she popped her head around her bedroom door a few minutes later.

'Can I borrow your beach wrap, love? Daniel and I are going down to the beach. I guess he'll take his mobile phone as usual if anyone needs him.'

Naomi murmured some acknowledgement and returned her attention immediately to her heroine's and hero's love story as Cindy grabbed the towelling robe to cover the bikini.

Daniel's eyes sparkled at her when she joined him.

'Spoilsport,' he murmured as he held his car door open for her.

She chose to ignore him but was thankful he refrained from any further comment, even when she at last took off the robe at the beach.

Cindy forgot all about her own lack of clothing when Daniel pulled his T-shirt over his head. His body was beautiful, simply beautiful.

He gave a muffled groan, and then she felt a finger under her chin. 'Don't look at me like that unless... unless...' His muttered words faded as her dazed eyes met his suddenly brilliant ones.

Suddenly he pulled her up against that tanned, firm body. Her arms automatically went around him, and then his lips were hot on her own, seeking, demanding the response that she willingly gave.

The sound of the surf and the voices of the families playing on the white sand receded. There was only the warmth of the body pressed to hers and the touch of his mouth on hers, and all the remembered heat and passion swept through her...

Cindy felt bereft when he suddenly moved abruptly, his lips leaving hers once again with that empty feeling while his hands moved to her upper arms and he pushed her abruptly away. Only then did she hear the wolf-whistles and cat-calls from a group of teenagers walking past them.

He took a step back as embarrassment swept through her. Cindy looked anywhere but at his face until he gave a muffled curse and grabbed her hand.

'I hope that blue water's as good as a cold shower,' he muttered.

She gave a startled gurgle of laughter and looked around. Kissing on the beach like a pair of teenagers had never been her style even when a teenager! A few folk not too far away were gaping at them, but they hastily turned their heads away as they saw her looking at them. Then she yielded to Daniel's tug on her hand and they were racing joyously towards the ocean. . .

As her fingers tightened around his strong hand she knew that he had definitely noticed the way she had reacted to his wide, warm expanse of bare flesh!

Perhaps not a front row forward's body after all, she thought helplessly as he at last let her go and splashed joyfully ahead of her to dive under the foaming crest of an incoming breaker, more like one of those bronzed, god-like surf lifesavers!

The water was delightfully cool against her hot skin, but after several minutes Cindy thought it wise to lie on the sand instead. She was unpleasantly surprised at how quickly she still became breathless after any real exertion. As she wiped herself with her beach towel Daniel ran up to her.

His muscles flowed and rippled under that gorgeous firm brown skin as he plunged through the soft sand. As he came closer Cindy managed to drag her gaze away from his body and then saw the question and concern in his eyes.

Before he could speak she said quickly, 'I'm fine, Daniel. Please, you have a decent swim. I'm quite happy to do a little sun-baking.'

'Well, don't overdo it this time.'

He hesitated a moment longer, then nodded, swiped his hands down his dripping wet, gleaming body and raced back to frolic and swim energetically in the surf. She watched him for a while, longing to be able to join him, but she was stretched out on her back when he at last returned.

Cindy resisted the temptation to watch him dry himself before he collapsed beside her.

'That was gorgeous,' he said with a sigh. 'It's been too long since I—'

He was silent. After a few moments Cindy stirred and yielded to the temptation to sit up and look at the long, strong body so near her.

'It's been too long since you what?' she prompted him softly. 'Had a holiday, even a few hours off from responsibility?'

'No,' he said at last after such a long silence that Cindy thought he intended to ignore her. 'It's been a long time since I felt so alive. I've always loved this beach.'

'If you like it here why did you take so long to come back?'

He sat up and, stretching out his long legs, leaned back on his hands and said pensively, 'During my first year as a resident I thought I'd like to be a surgeon, but by the end of my second year in the surgical ward. . .' He pulled a face and looked across at her. 'Why do you want to be a GP?'

'Because I found I like to be really involved with my patients.'

She knew his reason had been the same when he nodded briefly, not taking his eyes from her.

She continued quickly, 'In hospital, especially those really large city ones, it was far too easy for a person just to become a case and not someone who was a father, a mother, a child.' She hesitated, and then added softly, 'And one day, if I ever have a family, I thought it would be easier to take time out when they needed me.'

Daniel was silent for a long moment. 'Sally said the same thing, but it didn't work out like that.'

There was a trace of bitterness in his voice, and Cindy sat a little straighter.

'Surely you've already seen these last eighteen months or so that general practices can keep us as busy, if not more so, than hospital work?' He gave a rather grim laugh. 'If you're not careful sometimes you can get too involved in your patients' lives, too close to them.'

Cindy asked carefully, 'Why did you and Sally start your own practice in western Sydney instead of joining your father?'

Daniel stared out beyond the tumbling surf to the sparkling, deep blue waters, stretching to the horizon. 'Once I realised that I wanted my patients to be more than that appendectomy or that bowel cancer I started my family medicine training. Sally and I met just as she was finishing hers.

'Unfortunately, Dad and Sally didn't really get on together. She was a very driven person, and thought he was clinging to far too many methods that she considered outdated. She also wasn't keen on the nearest hospital being so far away as she wanted to work with women, especially obstetric work. After she died our practice was in too much financial trouble for it to be wise to dispose of it immediately.'

He stopped abruptly, ran his hand around the back of his neck and gave a short laugh. 'I don't know what it is about you, Cindy. I haven't mentioned Sally for months and then the first day we met, and now twice in one day, I've talked about her to you. You sure must be a hell of a doctor.'

Cindy watched him spring to his feet and pick up the beach towel he had been sitting on.

'Perhaps you need to talk about her, Daniel,' she offered hesitantly.

He looked at her sharply. 'It's been three years,' he said abruptly. 'She's just a part of my past now.'

And Cindy knew he did not want to talk about his wife any more.

As they made their way back to the car park Cindy suspected strongly that he was wrong. Whatever had happened to Sally, whatever their marriage had been like, she was anything but relegated to Daniel's past. And Brittany was his living, constant reminder of that fact.

CHAPTER SIX

CINDY's strength gradually improved each day and so Daniel reluctantly let her work longer hours, but sometimes by the end of a very busy day she was still very tired—something she did her best to hide from him. But although he did not say anything she knew he was not easily fooled, especially on one particularly busy day when he agreed to his father doing the house calls to a couple of his favourite old patients.

So Cindy had very mixed feelings when she was at last told that Andrew would hopefully be home on the following Monday, and the two elderly people had been persuaded to fly back the Thursday before to Canberra to pick up their camper-van and continue their trip to Victoria.

She knew that as soon as Aileen was home for good there would no longer be any excuse for her to stay in the same house as Daniel. Naomi would be gone and she would move at last into her own flat and would no longer see as much of him—and Brittany. Strangely, living by herself in the attractive flat the Burstons had arranged for her had lost its appeal.

Cindy tried to convince herself that it was only because having the three children in the house had brought back loving memories of when she had been at home with a baby sister and the constant coming and going of family members.

But deep in her soul she knew there was far more to it than that.

A certain tall, dark and handsome man had brought something alive in her when she was in his vicinity that she had never experienced before.

Mrs Burston had been fairly pleasant towards Cindy. However, she had kept her distance, and Cindy knew that for some reason she seemed to disapprove of her. Several times Cindy had seen her looking at Daniel with evident concern.

They left right after morning surgery and a quick lunch. Daniel was helping his father load their luggage into the car when Cindy said goodbye to his mother.

Mrs Burston took the hand Cindy offered, but instead of shaking it she suddenly held it between both of hers and looked earnestly at Cindy.

'Cindy, I'm very glad you're here, but I. . . I. . .' She hesitated and then said in a rush, 'You are a lovely woman but will you please be gentle with my son and granddaughter?'

Cindy stiffened, and the hands holding hers tightened.

'I'm sorry. I know it's none of my business.' Mrs Burston smiled a little crookedly but Cindy saw the worry in her eyes. 'Except that Daniel is my son and he has been hurt badly in the past. He and Sally had some major problems even before she became sick. You are obviously a dedicated doctor, a career woman like her, and I—'

The front door burst open. 'Grandma! Dad said hurry up or you'll miss the plane.'

Mrs Burston hesitated, but gave Cindy's hands another squeeze, before letting her go and hurrying off after Brittany. The little girl was dancing with excitement at having a day off school to go with them to the airport.

Cindy slowly followed and smiled a little blindly at Daniel as he strode towards her.

'For a wonder there are no house calls left to do, seeing that Dad insisted on doing those two this morning, and I'll be back in plenty of time to take the evening surgery, Cindy.' Daniel hesitated, before adding softly, 'Seeing

Aileen's taken Susan and Will in to visit Andrew, why don't you go to the beach with Naomi for a while?'

The sudden grin and teasing glint in his eyes told her he was remembering the red bikini and their own brief time at the beach. 'Here, take the mobile phone and let Jennifer ring you for any emergency.'

She avoided his eyes, which she had found she was doing quite a lot lately.

'I might just do that,' she agreed brightly, but her smile vanished as she waved them off.

The car had hardly disappeared before Naomi said quietly, 'Why don't you do what he said, rather than work at the flat as you had planned, Cindy?'

Cindy took a deep breath. 'Because, with any luck, that's where I will be living in another couple of days,' she said briskly, 'and I'd like to have it sorted out before you go home. School holidays will be starting very soon and apparently our workload increases dramatically with the influx of holiday-makers over Christmas and New Year.'

Naomi turned away abruptly. 'No,' she said flatly after a brief pause, 'this is the first time I've had a chance to go to the beach for quite a while without the kids.'

Cindy looked at her with surprise. 'But there's nothing to stop you going by yourself. I'll be fine.'

'Oh, no, you won't. And neither will I be if I let you finish that unpacking by yourself, lifting those remaining heavy boxes,' Naomi said grimly.

She scowled at Cindy's raised eyebrows, and then laughed. 'Two huge men will descend on me! Casey made me promise to make you behave, and Daniel told me to take you to the beach with me if I had to tie you down and drag you there!'

'Oh, did they just?' Cindy began indignantly. 'Just how old do they think I am?'

'Not old enough to look after yourself properly, I'd say.'

The sisters looked at each other for a moment and then laughed.

'Oh, well,' Cindy said reluctantly, 'the beach certainly does sound better than a blast from two huge men. But I do have to settle into the flat in the next couple of days,' she warned. 'As soon as Andrew's home I'll be living there.'

She refused point-blank to wear the bikini again. Despite Naomi's grumbles, they went to the flat and found her own one-piece costume. Even then Cindy felt ridiculously self-conscious of the lack of material covering her thighs, exposing them almost to the waist on each leg.

The day was perfect. There was not a cloud in the sky but the sun was not too hot and the surf was just right. There was a gentle breeze and for some reason there were not too many people about.

'Probably doing their kids' Christmas shopping before school breaks up in a couple of weeks,' Naomi mused, reminding Cindy that she had still not given much thought at all yet to that special day.

So the morning should have been perfect, but Cindy felt restless. After body-surfing a few waves and going for a brief swim Cindy left Naomi to it and spread out her towel in the shade of a tree near the edge of the sand.

Only when she was lying face down on it, with her eyes tightly closed, did she at last acknowledge to herself what was missing.

Daniel Burston was what was missing.

She groaned softly.

That attraction that had sprung up between them that first day had been kept carefully in check, especially with his parents around. But he was constantly in her thoughts, and she suddenly wished desperately that he could have joined her in playing in the tumbling waves and then be stretched out beside her here again on the sand.

She sat up and clasped her arms around her knees. Never had she dreamt that when she started falling in love with someone it would happen so spontaneously, so quickly. And it wasn't welcome. Not welcome at all. Especially if he. . .if he did not feel the same way about her.

And for some reason his mother did not like her. Or was there some other reason for her words and attitude? What had his mother been talking about this morning? Did she really give the impression she was such a dedicated career woman?

As the years had passed she had begun to wonder rather wistfully if she would ever fall in love. Certainly no man she had ever met had stirred her to the depths that Daniel Burston had.

And was it possible that she could possibly affect Daniel in the same way? she wondered wistfully.

She straightened a little. His mother had definitely inferred that Cindy had the power to hurt Daniel. Her heart suddenly lifted, and then plummeted again.

So what if he was attracted to her? After all, quite a few men over the years had been attracted to her shapely figure, had even kissed her. . .

She shivered and hugged herself tightly.

And she had been attracted to other men but no one's kiss had ever haunted her like Daniel Burston's, even if he had shown no sign of wanting to kiss her again. Obviously, he must have loved his wife deeply to be so hurt by her death.

And then, of course, there was Brittany.

'Admit it, Cindy,' she groaned out loud, 'you've also fallen for one small, independent, lovable, antagonistic girl!'

Brittany had been a different child since her grandparents had arrived. She had hardly let her grandmother out of her sight and, although still reserved with Cindy, had been the very lovable, happy and carefree child a girl of her age should be. And Cindy's heart had gone out to the motherless child who was so obviously hungry for love and approval.

Cindy was not at all happy with her thoughts and was glad when she saw Naomi coming out of the surf towards her.

'The undertow's getting too strong out there,' Naomi said breathlessly. 'The lifesaver on duty said the tide runs out very fast here sometimes. Said to watch for rips so I'll sun-bake for awhile.'

'You're very brown already, Naomi,' Cindy began to remonstrate, but stopped short at her sister's groan.

'I know, I know. The risk of melanomas, skin cancers! Daniel already read me the riot act that first day at letting you get so sunburnt! He didn't even give me a chance to explain how many lectures I've had already from the medicos in this family.'

She paused, and Cindy joined in chorus with her, 'As well as from Mum!'

They both grinned, and Cindy held her peace as Naomi stretched out in the full sun to dry. The trouble was that even when people knew the dangers they still often chose to ignore them on the premise that those kind of things happened to other people.

Naomi was silent and Cindy willed herself to a blissful mindlessness.

Then Naomi said softly in a muffled voice, 'Cindy, Mum rang when you were at the surgery last night and wants me back home to help her.'

A pang touched Cindy. Christmas was very close. Traditionally the whole family descended on their parents each year. More and more in recent years it had been the only day they could all be home together. Even during her training she had been fortunate enough to be able to get home for some part of the day.

'I don't know if I'll be able to make it this year for Christmas, Naomi,' Cindy said slowly. 'This place apparently becomes inundated with holiday-makers. Christmas Day, and morc cspccially Boxing Day, is oftcn thc busiest time of the year here in the practice. And with Andrew still out of action. . .'

Naomi sat up slowly. 'Don't you think Daniel would let you go if you told him about Dad?'

The sadness that filled Cindy was reflected in Naomi's face.

'It's three years now since Dad was diagnosed with multiple myeloma and he's really doing very well,' Cindy said swiftly.

Naomi hesitated, and Cindy straightened. 'Has something happened, Naomi?' she asked sharply.

Tears filled the eyes so much like her own, and Cindy caught her breath with fear.

'His. . .his last bone marrow test wasn't too good. Mum said he's out of remission and has to start another course of chemotheraphy tomorrow.'

Cindy stared at her for a moment and then gazed blindly away across the blue, tumbling surf.

So now it had started up all over again. The trips to the oncology unit in Newcastle, the side-effects of the treatment, the prayers that the therapy would work once more and that this time. . .this time he would go into remission again.

She had thought her father had looked rather tired, but had hoped it might be because of his worry over her own illness and her impatience with her mother's fussing. That had been another reason why she had been so glad to go home with Casey.

'Does Casey know?'

'Mum was going to ring him as soon as I hung up,

but she asked me not to tell you straight away. Today would do, she said. Casey did ring last night and said he'd pick me up this afternoon and take me home. He wants to see Dad for himself.'

Cindy sighed and pushed herself to her feet. 'Typical of Mum. Her philosophy has always been to let a person have a good night's sleep if at all possible and then tell them bad news. No wonder you wanted your last swim.'

Naomi looked a little guilty. 'I couldn't resist it, and you needed to relax, too, Cindy,' she said gently.

Cindy forced a smile. 'You've looked after me very well, sister mine. I guess we'd better go home and pack your things now, though. Knowing Casey, he'll probably arrive early and may even be waiting for us.'

She hesitated, and then asked quietly, 'Does Daniel know?'

Naomi stood too. 'Not unless Aileen told him. I waited up and told her as soon as she came home last night, but you and Daniel had already gone to bed. That's one reason she took the kids with her today. She said she'll be able to manage fine. Now she knows Andrew will be home in a few days she won't spend as much time at the hospital.'

She paused and chewed on her lip as she surveyed Cindy. 'Cindy, there's one thing I've been meaning to say. I've only met Jennifer Coats a couple of times, but be careful of her, would you? From a few things Brittany has said I know that the woman doesn't like you.'

Cindy pulled a face. 'Yeah, I've kind of gathered that.' She frowned. 'But I have no real idea why.'

Naomi gave a laugh. 'Oh, Cindy, you're so dumb sometimes. She's just like a girl at school I knew. Even if she didn't want to go out with a guy herself she still hated it when he ignored her. I'd say Daniel's ignored her and it's hurt her pride when you come along and, bingo, the man fusses over you not working too hard and can hardly keep his eyes off you.'

Daniel couldn't keep his eyes off her?

Cindy's mouth stretched into a delighted smile and she was glad Naomi was busy shaking sand from her towel.

'So, Cindy, you're free to go to your flat at last. I did most of my packing last night. It's your stuff we've got to pack.'

Her smile faded and a sharp pang swept through Cindy, as well as a sense of loss. She had spent her last day close to Daniel, her last night under the same roof. And she wondered suddenly if Daniel would mind. Really mind. Even miss her. Probably not, she thought wistfully.

But one thing was certain. She knew him well enough now to realise that Dr Daniel Burston would certainly mind not having been told what was going on.

And she was right.

But first she had to endure Casey and Naomi transferring her belongings to her flat and helping her to finish sorting out the place.

Over the past few days Cindy and Naomi had spent a little time at the flat, doing some unpacking, so it did not really take them very long. Casey arrived with boxes of groceries and Naomi insisted on helping move all Cindy's things from the Sacks' house and fussed around, settling her in, until Cindy felt like screaming.

She was very thankful for her twin's perception when he said firmly at last, 'Right, that's enough, Naomi. I'm sure Cindy would rather potter around by herself now, otherwise she won't know where anything is, and we don't want to arrive at Mum and Dad's too late tonight.'

After they had gone the small flat felt cold and lonely.

Having been reared in a noisy, full home of seven people, she had always enjoyed the quietness and peace of living by herself. Since the arrival of Daniel's parents there had been constant comings and goings, and now she realised just how she had thrived on it all.

She did potter around for a while, but Naomi had even insisted on making up her bed and there was really little left to do except finish unpacking her clothes, sort out the pile of wall hangings and ornaments and decide how to arrange them.

She made herself a cup of tea. Then she decided she would have to go back to the Sacks' house and wait for Daniel so she could explain. She would hate him to think she had just moved out without a word.

'Who are you trying to fool, woman?' she muttered as she slammed the door behind her and hurried the few yards around the corner to the large house at the back of the medical centre. 'You just want an excuse to be home when he arrives and, worse—just to see the man, like an adolescent fan!'

But she had left it too late. Daniel's sleek black car was already parked in the driveway. As she walked up the path he stormed out of the front door and down the steps.

When he spotted her he stood stock-still. The expressions that flitted across his face astonished and then confused her. She thought she saw immense relief, but that was swallowed up by the fury that filled his eyes and voice.

'So you do have the grace to come and explain!' he exploded.

'Explain?' Her voice sounded squeaky with surprise, and she swallowed hard to dislodge the sudden lump in her throat.

He came closer and grabbed her by both arms. Her skin burnt where he touched her.

Would his touch always scald her? she wondered helplessly as she stared up into his angry face.

He looked intently at her and disappointment replaced some of the anger in his eyes. 'Couldn't you have told *me* you hated staying here and were fed up with us all, instead of packing up the minute my back's turned and just clearing out like this?'

There was a movement behind him and Cindy stared at Brittany as she appeared on the veranda. There was frank triumph on her small face.

Cindy stared at the small girl thoughtfully for a long moment and uncertainty replaced the triumph.

Then she glanced back up at Daniel. 'Let me go, Daniel,' she said very softly.

For a moment his hands tightened and then, as though he suddenly realised what he was doing, he let her go abruptly and took a step back.

She looked up at him as calmly as she could, hoping he could not see the turbulence inside her that his touch and closeness were generating.

'What on earth makes you think I've hated staying here and being so closely involved with your family?'

He looked uncertain for a moment, but Brittany suddenly darted forward and said in a shrill voice, 'Auntie Aileen said so! She told Naomi she could quite understand how her sister must be sick to death of the lot of us.'

'Well, your aunt was very much mistaken, Brittany. I'm a member of a large family who love each other and I have been made to feel very welcome by *almost* every member of your family. I've very much enjoyed living here with you all,' she said very firmly.

She kept her eyes fixed on Brittany who, after a moment, had the grace to hang her head.

She heard Daniel draw in a swift breath, and when she dared to look at him he was staring at Brittany. He looked swiftly at Cindy. There was sudden comprehension in his face. His eyes flashed and he opened his mouth, but closed it again at the swift shake of her head.

'I'm sure Naomi must have told Aileen how wrong she was. She knows how fond I've become of you all,' said Cindy briskly, and knew she was right by the look Brittany flashed guiltily at her.

Daniel stiffened. 'Brittany, if you repeat something you overhear it is very important that you report all of it so that someone does not get the wrong idea.' A steely note had entered his voice, and Brittany's eyes widened. 'If you don't it becomes the same thing as telling lies. Do I make myself clear?'

There was a snap to his voice and Brittany took a step back. 'Well, *I* hate having her here, so there!'

She swung away and raced off, but not before Cindy had seen the tears in her defiant eyes.

Daniel moved as though to call her back but, instead, swung his dark gaze towards Cindy. 'What the hell's the matter with her?'

Cindy bit her lip. How could she tell him that his daughter was jealous of him showing any attention to her, without him thinking she was making a play for him, and, even worse, that she had taken his kiss far more seriously than he had and that she suspected his daughter somehow sensed it.

'Cindy, what's been going on with you and Brittany? What have you done to upset her?'

'Me upset *her*!'

Cindy felt the hurt and confusion of the talk with his mother and the pain of her father's illness whelm up, and controlled herself with difficulty.

'I suggest you ask your daughter. If you can't work it out for yourself, that is,' she said curtly, and turned to walk away.

He moved in front of her. 'You still haven't told me why you've shifted out without a word.'

Cindy looked back at him warily. Would this be a good time to mention her father's illness and ask for Christmas off? No, she decided, it would be best to wait and see how Andrew was closer to the day.

Instead she shrugged and said, 'Mum rang up last night and told Naomi she needed her at home. Aileen said she could manage now and so there was no point in waiting any longer to move to the flat.'

Something like hurt flashed across his face. 'Aileen knew? Why didn't you tell me?'

'I didn't know myself until after you'd gone,' she said wearily. 'Naomi took the message and told Aileen last night. In fact, Naomi didn't see fit to tell me until after she'd had her last swim. Casey picked her up a little while ago. They both insisted on helping me move my things.'

They stared at each other for a moment.

'I'm going to miss you,' he murmured quietly.

Not half as much as I'm going to miss you, she wanted to cry back, but instead she took a deep breath and said just as quietly, 'I think it's just as well I won't be around night and day to aggravate your daughter any more.'

He frowned quickly. 'I don't know what's come over her. She said that very first day how much she liked you.'

Cindy hesitated, and then took a deep breath. 'Has she ever seen you kiss anyone since her mother died?'

Startled awareness leapt into his face, but before he could answer she nervously tucked a handful of hair behind one ear and said briskly, 'It's really nothing to do with me. I just called around to tell you what has happened and. . .and. . .' She tried frantically to think of some excuse and then said triumphantly, 'And to pick up my bunch of surgery keys I left behind.'

'Have tea with us tonight.'

She ignored the plea in his eyes, shook her head and said with forced cheerfulness, 'Casey stocked up my fridge with so much food I'd better start on it before it goes off.'

The meat and vegetable casserole her sister-in-law had

sent with Casey was delicious. But while she was trying to eat it in her new kitchen later that evening Cindy acknowledged glumly that it was the loneliest meal she had ever had. She would even have welcomed Brittany's glowering looks across the table from her.

That thought made her smile and then frown.

Daniel's obvious astonishment and dismay with his daughter had highlighted the fact of Brittany's usual honesty. It had revealed only too clearly the depths of her determination to cause trouble for Cindy.

Having that small girl dislike her so much had done dreadful things to her sense of self-esteem, and she spent the rest of the evening trying to work out some way she could convince Daniel's daughter that she presented no threat whatsoever to Brittany's relationship with her father.

But it was thoughts of the father, not the daughter, that filled Cindy's thoughts while she tossed and turned, trying to get to sleep. She had not realised just how much she would miss spending time alone with Daniel after his parents had gone home and Naomi and the children were in bed. They had got into the habit of having a last cup of tea together, discussing the patients and activities of the children during the day.

It was in the darkest hour of the night that Cindy at last admitted just how much she loved Daniel Burston, that she would always love him and would be devastated and always miss him if he went out of her life.

And there was every chance of that, she acknowledged sadly.

There was so much about Daniel she still longed to know. She had gathered that his marriage had not been without its problems, but the mere fact that he never talked about his wife had shown her that his love for her must have been deep and strong.

She dwelt sadly on that for a while. But then, strangely

enough, the mere admission to herself about the depth of her feelings for Daniel brought a sense of peace, and she at last fell asleep.

CHAPTER SEVEN

THE next morning Cindy drew a deep, deep breath before she pushed open the door to the medical centre, and breathed a sigh of relief when Jennifer raised her head and observed a little too sharply, 'First for once, Dr James.'

'And good morning to you, too, Miss Coats,' she retorted smartly.

The receptionist had the grace to flush slightly, but before she could respond the outside door banged open and Daniel strode in.

Cindy tensed as she turned to greet him. The ferocious scowl on his face dried up any attempt she might have made to speak to him. He barely nodded at Cindy, barked a curt greeting as he strode past and, without stopping, just as curtly asked Jennifer to let him know the moment his first patient arrived.

He looked as though he had slept as little as Cindy had. Her heart leapt. Had he missed her as much as she had missed him? Then she slumped. He'd probably been called out to a patient during the night.

Jennifer stared after him with wide eyes. 'What's bitten him this morning?' she muttered crossly.

Cindy quickly moved past her to her own room, pretending she hadn't heard, and while she waited for her first patient she forced herself to concentrate on studying the medical histories of the first few patients she would see.

With some relief, she noted that the first few should be straightforward enough. A middle-aged woman had booked for a vaginal smear test. Sutures were due to be removed from a teenager. Good. Jennifer could do that one after she had checked the wound.

One elderly woman with chronic asthma would hopefully only need her chest checked and prescriptions renewed.

But the next one was a two-and-a-half-year-old child, with no note from Jennifer to say what the mother had stated was wrong.

Cindy noted that the birth had been attended by Andrew in an emergency situation at home, after which the baby was transferred to hospital by ambulance with the mother. The baby had been brought in quite regularly since birth. Some appointments had been for check-ups and help for the mother with breast-feeding in the early days.

Cindy frowned. Breast-feeding had been abandoned early, even though Andrew had noted how upset the mother had been. The baby had then apparently thrived, but there seemed to have been more than the usual baby ailments.

The last visit had been a few months before. Andrew had noted that the mother was still having problems with the infant not eating and sleeping properly. The toddler was again underweight and exceedingly restless, even screaming constantly while being examined.

No evident problem had been detected but Andrew had given the mother anti-colic medication and helpful brochures on behavioural problems. He had written in his untidy scrawl two large question marks before 'More than poor parenting?' He had also noted that he had asked the mother to return for a follow-up visit in a month, or immediately if she was still having problems.

Cindy frowned. Obviously Andrew had doubts that it was only a management problem, but the mother had not returned until now.

Cindy's heart sank when the father followed the

woman into her office. The squirming, screaming boy was held firmly in his arms and he threw Cindy a very belligerent look. His wife was pale and exhausted, far too thin and tense.

'Where's Dr Sack?' the man snapped above the noise his son was making.

'I'm sorry, but he is hospitalised himself,' Cindy said loudly. 'Mr and Mrs Nichols? How do you do? I'm Dr James. This is John?' Mr Nichols nodded abruptly and she added, 'What can I do for you?'

'Shut this brat up for one!'

The woman burst into noisy tears at her husband's furious words, and the 'brat' screamed louder.

Cindy stared at the tense figure of the small boy, now sitting on his father's knee. He was pushing at his father's large hands, holding himself rigidly away from contact with his father.

'Oh, do put him down, Tom! You know he is always quieter when he's on the floor,' the woman cried wearily, dashing at the tears on her cheeks.

A look of hurt crossed the man's face, and Cindy revised her immediate fear of child abuse as he snarled, 'With pleasure.' He plonked the boy down on the carpet beside him.

The mother quickly put a large, rather battered teddy-bear on the floor in front of her son, which he made no attempt to reach for. The boy screamed a few more times but suddenly stopped. His thumb went into his mouth and he started rocking quickly backward and forwards. The man snorted with disgust and crossed his arms.

Margaret Nichols crooned softly, 'There, Johnny, that's a good boy.' She looked up ashamedly at Cindy. 'I'm sorry, Doctor, he really is a good boy. It's just that he hates strange places and loud noises.'

The infant was staring down at the teddy-bear while still rocking. The rocking was gradually slowing, but was still rhythmical rocking. Cindy watched him for a moment, and then something clicked in her mind.

To hide her face she looked down at the notes in front of her. Those large question marks showed that perhaps Andrew had also begun to suspect what the problem might be, although he had not noted his suspicions. Not very often was a diagnosis of this problem made under thirty months of age.

'I see that Dr Sack asked you to return if you were still having problems,' she asked quietly. 'Have the problems started up again, Mrs Nichols?'

The woman hesitated, and her husband said loudly, 'There was nothing really wrong with him before.'

The rocking motion increased and the child started crying again.

'Oh, hush, Tom, you know when you talk too loud it makes him worse,' Mrs Nichols said tearfully but in a very soft murmur.

Cindy's heart sank further, but she stood up and moved her chair a little distance away from her desk. 'I think it would be better if we left young John in peace. Would you like to move over to this side of the room away from him?'

After they were settled again Mr Nichols said in a low, taut voice, 'I've been trying to tell my wife she spoils him too much. She's got to be firmer with him.'

Mrs Nichols's eyes filled with tears again, but she muttered angrily, 'You don't know what it's like, day in, day out. You're away most of the time and you don't know a thing about him. I've been trying to tell you there's something wrong.'

Cindy intervened quickly. 'I see here in Dr Sack's notes that you've a long history of feeding and sleeping problems with him, Mrs Nichols. I know how exhausting that must be for you,' she said sympathetically.

Mrs Nichols sat up a little straighter and dabbed at her

wet cheeks. 'Last time Dr Sack gave me all kinds of things to read about parenting and early childhood,' she began, but her husband interrupted again.

'And that was a waste of time—and money! We've already raised two daughters. They've taught us more than those damned so-called experts. We never had any of these problems with them,' he said belligerently. 'All those articles did was convince you we are bad parents after all.'

'Oh, no, I'm quite sure Dr Sack did not want you to think that at all, Mr Nichols,' Cindy said firmly. 'Now,' she continued briskly, 'I'd like to ask you a few questions about his general development.'

A few moments later she put down her pen, excused herself and went to Daniel's room. She was thankful that he had no patient with him.

'Daniel, could I have a moment, please?'

He looked up from writing in a chart and smiled crookedly at her. 'You must have a serious problem to risk being snapped at. According to Jennifer, I've been rather, er, cranky.'

Cindy smiled gently back at him. 'I didn't think that would last very long.'

Something lit up in his eyes. 'Well, my first patient didn't seem too happy with me, I was informed rather strongly by our redoubtable receptionist,' he said ruefully. His eyes darkened and he said quietly, 'I missed having breakfast with you.'

Cindy drew in a breath and the words flew out before she could stop them. 'I missed you more last night at supper.'

He was very still for a moment. They stared at each other, and Cindy said huskily, 'Forget I said that, please.'

She cleared her throat and added rapidly, before he could speak, 'I've got a couple of worried parents and a two-and-a-half-year-old child I'd like you to see.'

'You're a very good doctor, Cindy, and a very good general practitioner.'

Cindy's eyes widened at his praise. She suddenly felt ridiculously pleased that the man she loved thought so highly of her.

Daniel smiled gently at her. 'It's true, and this is really the first time you've come to me for any help. We haven't even had time to schedule any formal discussion sessions.'

'I can assure you it won't be the last time I need help,' Cindy said fervently. 'There's always so much to learn.'

He snorted. 'That goes for both of us.' His dark eyes blazed at her suddenly. 'Right now I'd much rather learn more about you, Cindy James, than medicine.'

And I about Daniel Burston, she wanted to cry out, but Cindy fought for control. Why on earth did he have to choose to talk to her like that when her mind had been trying to concentrate on. . .?

'Daniel, I'd like to indulge, too, but right now I've got very worried parents waiting for me with their son.'

His face suddenly went cold. 'Of course, your patient has to come first. What have you got?'

She hated the sudden loss of warmth, but swallowed hard, still trying not to yield to her own pressing desire to talk to him about their own relationship.

Briefly and concisely she filled him in. Even as a baby John had stiffened and cried when cuddled. He was much happier when no one tried to touch him. At times he seemed to his parents to live in his own little world. He was still not making any attempts to speak, although he seemed to have very acute hearing, and he had only recently started to walk.

Other behaviour that the mother especially considered 'odd' was that they had worked out that he would only willingly eat bright-coloured food, especially anything red. The last point Cindy mentioned was the mother's claim that when the father came home after being away for a few days with his trucking business the child seemed much worse, with severe tantrums.

'She claims young John doesn't like his routines changed at all, and that these last couple of months he seems to be getting much worse,' Cindy finished rapidly. 'Could you come and have a peep at him?'

'Of course.' Daniel stood up slowly, looking thoughtfully at Cindy. 'You do know what classic symptoms you've been describing, don't you?'

'Yes, I'm afraid I do,' she said sadly, 'but I want you to see the child yourself first.'

After Cindy had introduced Daniel to the very subdued parents Daniel stood and watched John, rocking backwards and forwards.

At last he asked, 'Has this rocking been getting worse?'

Mrs Nichols hesitated, but her husband said gruffly, 'Every time I've been away for more than a few days I reckon he's worse. Not only in that constant movement either. And he still doesn't talk!'

Daniel looked at Cindy and nodded. 'Do you know a good referral?'

She hesitated and then a slight smile tilted her lips. 'I do, as a matter of fact, unless there is someone else you would prefer. But Dr Benjamin James, a very caring paediatrician I've known for a long time, has had experience with this particular problem.'

Surprise lit Daniel's eyes. 'You've been withholding information, Dr James,' he said softly. 'I'm sure that if you suggest him he must be good.'

He turned to the strained, anxious faces of the parents. 'We think it's possible your son may have a problem called autism,' he said very gently, 'but we would like you to see a specialist to have it confirmed. I have a patient waiting for me so I'll leave Dr James to explain to you.'

After he had gone Cindy spent some time talking to the shocked parents, telling them about autism and what little was known about it.

'It's basically a condition in which a child is unable to relate to people and situations, and may show an obsessive resistance to change,' she concluded, and added quickly, anticipating the next question, 'The precise causes are unknown but evidence points to a physical basis, and it is likely that there is a subtle form of brain damage. The earlier theory that lack of warmth from parents was a cause is now rejected.'

Something like relief swept through both white faces.

'We've tried so hard, Doctor. Ever since he was born. We were so pleased we had our son at last, but it's been hard. . .'

The big, strong truck driver was close to tears and Cindy hastily interrupted. 'I'm sure you've been very good parents, both of you. In fact, you've done very well bringing him in to be checked out so early. If it is autism the sooner a diagnosis is made the better. Now, I want to write out a referral and make an appointment for John to see a specialist. Could one of you call in tomorrow and pick it up?'

There had been something else Cindy had been concerned about and was glad when Mrs Nichols offered eagerly to do that. Her husband hesitated for a moment and then nodded abruptly, before standing up.

Mrs Nichols went over quickly to gently pick up her son, and Cindy's soft heart ached for her as the child resisted. As the woman very slowly hoisted him onto her hip Cindy noticed again what looked like a bruise on the woman's wrist as her long sleeve fell back. Her mouth tightened. It was such a warm day that she had thought it unusual the woman had chosen to wear such a hot garment.

Daniel had also noticed. 'Did you see the long sleeves and high collar Mrs Nichols was wearing?' he asked abruptly when they met briefly after surgery.

'Yes,' Cindy said grimly, 'and they didn't altogether hide the bruises.'

His expression darkened. 'Did you tackle the husband?'

'No, I thought it better to wait until she was alone.'

'I'm not sure that was a good idea,' Daniel said slowly. 'From what you told me, he was ready for a fight with Andrew when he came in and you may not get him to the surgery again.'

'And if I'd tackled him about abusing his wife in front of her she would have instantly denied it!' Cindy sighed as he raised his eyebrows at her angry tone. 'I saw far too many women at my last practice who had been victims of domestic violence.'

Daniel snorted. 'There were far too many at our practice in the western suburbs of Sydney as well.'

'Did you find the women were more open to your wife than to you?' she asked quietly.

There was silence for a moment. Cindy risked a look at his face, and pain slashed her at the look of sadness on his face.

'I'm sorry, Daniel, I shouldn't have—'

He moved abruptly and she bit her lip. 'Yes, I did. Or at least she always claimed she saw more than I did. She had a thing about domestic violence. Apparently, she saw too much of it first hand when she was a kid. Her father was an alcoholic. She even set up a clinic and support group in our area for women and their kids. Spent a lot of time with them.'

The clipped words stopped abruptly. He stood up.

'Spent far more time there than I wanted her to,' he added harshly.

Cindy saw anger tighten his lips and said hesitantly, 'She must have been a very compassionate, caring woman.'

His expression hardened. 'Yes, Sally cared very much—for her patients,' he added, and then said abruptly 'There's only one house call after lunch and no surgery tonight. I promised Brittany I'd put in an appearance at the Christmas play she's in at school today. They are having it earlier than usual this year, for some reason or other.'

He paused for a moment, and said hesitantly, 'Cindy, I don't suppose you'd like to come with me?'

Cindy's heart was doing all kinds of things that none of her cardiology textbooks had ever mentioned. First it had ached for Daniel and the pain in him when she had mentioned his wife, and now it lurched dangerously at his invitation. She longed to go with him but she hesitated, wondering if her appearance would spoil Brittany's day.

'Please, Cindy, I hate being one of the only dads there.'

She couldn't resist the pleading in his voice. 'I'd love to go.' She forced a grin. 'It's been a long time since I went to one of Naomi's school dos with Mum.'

Pleasure lit up his face and he beamed at her. 'Great!'

As she and Daniel joined the audience in the school assembly hall Cindy hoped fervently that Brittany would think it was great having the woman she disliked so much accompany her father.

But, rather to Cindy's amazement, Brittany was pleased.

Her face was filled with excitement as she raced over to hug her father at the end of the performance.

'You were the best reindeer I've ever seen,' Daniel told her proudly.

She beamed, and then groaned, 'But that rotten horn thing would keep slipping off my head.'

'But you carried it all off with great talent.' Cindy smiled at her. 'The sign of a very good actor.'

'Cindy!'

Until that moment Cindy had not realised that Brittany was unaware of her, standing behind Daniel. She held her breath, waiting for the usual scowl.

Instead, a myriad emotions crossed Brittany's face. 'You came, too?' she asked, with such absolute amazement that Cindy caught her breath.

She smiled at the small girl. 'Wouldn't have missed your star performance for the world.'

'But aren't there any patients today?' Brittany asked with a puzzled look from Cindy to her father. 'Mum always said there were too many for her to come to my school things.'

Cindy saw Daniel stiffen. 'This is the country, sweetheart, not the city—remember?'

Cindy bit her lip as Brittany looked uncertain for a moment and then smiled shyly at her. 'Thank you for coming,' she said politely, and then looked up at her father.

'Get your bag, sweetheart,' he said gently. 'We'll wait for you outside.'

Cindy and Daniel were silent as they made their way through other groups of excited children and their parents. Daniel looked grim, and Cindy did not know what to say.

'Sally was always too busy for Brittany. I just didn't think she would remember.'

There was so much pain in the low, muttered words that Cindy slid her hand through his arm and squeezed it sympathetically.

Daniel's hand closed over hers. 'Right up until that last month Sally wouldn't give up her beloved patients, not even to spend time with me. She never spent much time with her daughter for all of her five years.' His face was bleak.

A few things suddenly fell into place for Cindy. His wife had been so career-orientated that it had left scars on both him and his daughter.

She hesitated and asked softly, 'What. . .what did she die from, Daniel?'

She felt the tall body against her tense.

'Acute leukaemia. At first we blamed her fatigue on the heavy workload she insisted on.' His voice was full of bitterness. 'She didn't tell me about the headaches and. . .and all the other symptoms. Within two months of being diagnosed she was gone.'

Cindy drew in her breath sharply. Before she could express her shock Brittany bounded up to them, and she numbly followed the tall man who was bending down lovingly to his small daughter as they walked to the car.

Cindy's heart went out to them both, and to the young woman only a little older than herself whose life had been cut so short. But she was a little puzzled. Daniel seemed to be blaming himself, or even Sally perhaps, in some way for her early death. Surely a professional like Sally must have suspected early there was something wrong with her.

There would have been sore throats, night sweats, perhaps even shortness of breath. Later there would have been the ulceration of the mouth, bleeding from the gums, bruising on the skin. Acute leukaemia did have a rapid onset and was more common among children and young adults under twenty-five years of age, but still. . .

Cindy sighed deeply. Like a lot of people, perhaps in the early stages Sally had not wanted to admit there could be something seriously wrong with her.

* * *

During the next week there were individual appointments with John Nichols's parents. After careful questioning his mother did admit that her husband had lost his temper, grabbed her by the arms and flung her across the room the day before their visit to the surgery.

'It was the very first time,' Margaret Nichols pleaded with tears in her eyes, 'and I'm not really sorry now because it did shock him enough to let me persuade him to bring John to see you again.'

Although she made all kinds of excuses for her husband—including the stress he'd been under at work—Cindy spent some very profitable minutes with the man on his visit, pointing out the terrible pressure his wife had been under almost since their son had been born. It was a very flushed and chastened truck driver who left her surgery.

The days continued to fly by. At Daniel's insistence, Andrew was still enjoying his convalescence, but very soon Cindy grimly realised fully why the town needed three full-time doctors during the tourist season.

With school holidays imminent, and especially with the Christmas to New Year break looming, many patients squeezed in appointments. There was also a steady stream of holiday-makers with ailments from food poisoning to all types of injuries.

'Getting plenty of practice inserting sutures, are we Dr James?'

Cindy looked up from her desk and pulled a face at Daniel's amused expression. 'You could say that again! If only people wouldn't take their glass bottles down to the beach, especially at night-time! Or at least have the decency not to get so drunk they smash them on the rocks so the tides scatter sharp weapons in the sand. I've lost track of how many feet I've stitched up.'

'Well, you can't say your first day at work here didn't serve as a warning of things to come.'

Cindy stilled. Heat swept through her. He had kissed her that first day, that first morning. . .

The regret and longing which suddenly filled her made her want to weep. He had not shown the least interest in wanting to kiss her again since she had taken up residence in her own flat. And each day that had passed had only intensified her loneliness, her longing to spend more time with him and his daughter.

A couple of times Aileen had invited her over for an evening meal. She had only been able to accept a couple of times, and had immensely enjoyed being able to play briefly with Susan and the even more mischievous Will.

But when she had at last returned to her lonely flat she had been forced to admit her deep disappointment that Daniel and Brittany had not been there as well.

'Of course, the conclusion of that little episode was rather pleasant, if I remember correctly.'

Cindy blinked at Daniel. The twinkle she loved so much sparkled at her from his dark eyes. Then his softly murmured words registered and she felt the sudden heat scorch her cheeks.

'You know, you do blush adorably,' that wretched, teasing murmur continued, 'especially for a woman who could face down that burly truck driver so well the other day when you spoke to him about losing his temper and taking it out on his wife.'

'Only you seem to have that effect on me,' she retorted, without thinking.

He gave a soft, rather startled chuckle. Cindy bent her head quickly over the notes on her desk.

Now why on earth had she told him that? She deliberately signed her name with her usual scrawl, and then reluctantly put her pen down.

Still avoiding looking at him, she said abruptly, 'Speaking of that truck driver, the Nichols's appointment with Ben was early this morning. He's heavily booked, but managed to fit their appointment in for us after his normal hours. Ben said he'd ring us when he had a chance. And, apparently, both parents have also agreed to counselling as well.'

Daniel didn't speak, and after a moment she reluctantly glanced up at him. He was eyeing her with a very thoughtful, rather grave look on his face. Their glances met and suddenly Cindy couldn't look away.

As though she had not spoken, he said in a voice taut with need, 'Cindy, there have been quite a few times when I've wanted very badly to kiss you again.'

His blunt, direct words almost took her breath away.

She stared back at him, and slowly stood up, not for a moment losing eye contact.

'Then why on earth haven't you?' she muttered angrily.

Daniel was very still for a moment, and then he smiled.

It was that glorious smile which started deep in his eyes and spread slowly all over his face before his lips moved at all, and always caused Cindy's heart to race madly.

He took a quick step and his strong arms reached for her. She was hauled up against his warm, strong body. There was a trace of spicy aftershave mingled with a lingering whiff of medical lotion.

Her arms automatically slid around his waist and as she leaned against him for one bewildering moment it felt like she had come home.

Their arms tightened around each other. She felt him take a deep breath, rested her head against his and closed her eyes. She loved the masculine scent of him, the strong hands that were moulding her to him tighter and tighter. . .

And then it wasn't enough.

Her arms slipped up around his thick, strong neck. As she had so many times longed to, her fingers moved through the curls at his nape. They looked so crisp, so strong, but they were soft, curling around her fingers as she felt the muscles there tense. Then he was pushing her away from him far enough to seek her mouth.

Her breath eased from her as their lips met, gently at first, nibbling—tasting each other—and then his lips captured hers.

The kiss deepened until it was full of hunger and passionate demand. His arms crushed her against his chest. She clung even tighter to him and the fire thrust through and around her and all rational thinking was swept away.

Timeless moments later he rested his head against her, his mouth still touching her forehead, and she felt humbled as she felt his strong body trembling.

Gradually their short, gasping breaths eased. She stirred, lifting a hand to cradle his cheek, and stared at him in wonder.

'That was some kiss, Dr Burston.'

He pressed a kiss into the palm of her hand, his eyes gleaming down at her. 'Oh, Dr James,' he mocked her in a voice that curled her fingers to cling even tighter, 'you ain't seen nuffin' yet!'

She grinned at the mimicking of his four-year-old niece and waited expectantly as he bent his head. But his lips only very gently touched hers, lingered for a moment and Cindy melted against him again as though her body had no will of its own.

He groaned. 'We do choose the worst places to do this,' he murmured.

'Well, it has been rather crowded with people around.' She smiled a little shyly at him.

'Yeah, it has been pretty crowded.' He grinned a little crookedly at her.

He looked a little pale and as shaken as she felt. A sudden wave of love for him flooded through her on a sweeping tide, but then it left her and suddenly she felt drained, anxious.

There was no doubt that he desired her. But what if he did not love her as she was certain she loved him? She had always vowed that a death-do-us-part marriage type of loving was all she would ever be prepared to settle for.

With a stab of pain she remembered suddenly what his mother had said. There was a far better chance that it would be Cindy who would be hurt!

'What is it, Cindy?'

Her hands fell to her side, but his hands slid up to her shoulder and tightened.

'Cindy? You looked so sad for a moment.'

'I do like your family, Daniel,' she said slowly, and pushed her hands against his chest.

His hands fell away and she took a step back.

He looked puzzled. 'What does my family have to do with kissing you? Why do I hear a "but" in there somewhere, Cindy?'

She hesitated, not sure what to say. How could she tell him about her anxiety over his mother's attitude towards her, and even more so how much his daughter's antagonism saddened and filled her with apprehension?

She looked around her helplessly. 'We. . .we shouldn't be doing this here. Anyone could have come in.'

She was thinking of Brittany as she spoke. He must have also for suddenly his body stiffened. Her eyes flew back to his face. For a moment a bleak look touched his passion-filled eyes.

Puzzled, she frowned, searching his eyes. Of its own volition one hand flew to linger on his cheek.

He stared at her for a long moment with a strange expression on his face, and then he relaxed. 'You women!' he murmured, 'you're all alike. Would it really matter if anyone saw us?'

Cindy stilled. With Sally's career ambitions she would never have wanted to be seen even kissing her own husband.

'No,' she whispered, 'it wouldn't matter a scrap.'

His face softened, and then such a tender, loving expression filled his face that all breath left her.

She must have swayed towards him. He closed the small gap between them again and their hands reached for each other.

And then they froze as they both heard the snap of the door from the waiting room and the clicking of high heels.

He swore softly and moved quickly away from her. 'I guess here comes one reason why you're right.'

His soft words were so cross, so rueful, that Cindy found herself laughing at him across the space he had put between them.

Perhaps no matter what he had said she would have laughed at that moment. Such a feeling of happiness and euphoria was flooding through her that she was almost dazed by it.

He loved her.

There had been no mistaking the love she had seen lighting up his face, and hope had filled her to overflowing.

CHAPTER EIGHT

THERE was a brief rap on the door. It opened and Jennifer put her head around the corner. Relief lit her anxious face and she entered the room quickly.

'Oh there you are, Daniel. I though you must have already gone. It's Joe Cooper. A bad turn while driving his car.'

Cindy saw an alert look enter Daniel's eyes. He rubbed his cheek slowly. 'Mr Cooper? Andrew told me about him, but he hasn't been into the surgery for a while, has he?'

Jennifer suddenly looked sharply from him to Cindy. Daniel had made some attempt to smooth back his short curls that her hands had ruffled. She had quickly tried to straighten her own blouse where long fingers had caressed, lingered. . .

Cindy stared back at the receptionist, wondering if she looked as well kissed as she felt. She lifted her head a little and forced herself to return the receptionist's suspicious gaze calmly.

'Jennifer?' Daniel said with a sudden snap in his voice.

'He missed his last appointment with Andrew,' Jennifer said, quickly turning back to him. 'Must be nearly six weeks at least. I didn't stop to find his chart before I called someone. He's in a lot of pain, looks terrible.'

The usually unflappable receptionist was a little pale, her words tumbling over each other.

Daniel was already on his way towards the door. He paused and looked back at Cindy. 'Perhaps you should come, too. Usually he sees his oncologist, but you may get a call out to his home some time. He's got multiple myeloma.'

After he had disappeared out the door Cindy squeezed her eyes tightly shut for a moment. The swing from such joy to pain confused her.

She had not come across another patient before with the same disease as her father, but she had always dreaded it. So that she could understand more what was happening with her father, she had read all she could about this disease that caused pain and destruction of bone tissue because of the proliferation and disordered function of plasma cells in the bone marrow.

She knew myeloma was rare, with only about six hundred cases diagnosed annually in Australia, and although the severity of the illness and the outlook varied only about one fifth of patients survived for four years or longer from the time of diagnosis.

And that last piece of information she had never mentioned to anyone in the family, although she had sometimes wondered if her mother had ever asked the doctors—or Benjamin even—about her husband's life expectancy. This could so very easily be his last Christmas with them.

But with ever-improving methods of treatment, the authorities had been proved wrong time and time again, she told herself fiercely.

Cindy brushed her hands across the moisture in her eyes and reluctantly made her way to Daniel's room. He was drawing up an injection near a grey-faced, sweating man. He was probably about fifty, much younger than her father.

Daniel frowned at her and murmured sharply, 'I thought you must have decided not to come.'

Out loud he said cheerfully, 'Joe Cooper, meet Dr James. You might be lucky enough to get the pretty doctor on one of your home visits.'

Mr Cooper nodded slightly at Cindy, without speaking, and Daniel continued quickly, 'Now, let's get this pain-killer into you. If you wouldn't mind placing that tourniquet for me, Cindy, so I can find a vein?'

Together they worked quickly and in a few minutes the pain started to ease, the frail body gradually relaxing.

With his fingers feeling the man's pulse, Daniel said quietly, 'Joe was diagnosed two years ago and has apparently been pretty good the last few months. Was on the way to visit his daughter when he developed severe pain in his abdomen and back. I've asked Jennifer to—Ah, here she is.'

'One on the way, stat, as ordered, Dr Burston.' Jennifer nodded meaningfully to Daniel. Her eyes flickered to Cindy, but she chose to ignore her. 'Anything else, Doctor?'

Mr Cooper said weakly, 'My daughter. . . She'll be worried. . .'

'And your wife? Is she at home today?' Daniel asked steadily.

Alarm flashed in the man's eyes. 'You don't have to bother her, surely?'

'Now, Mr Cooper, you know how your wife would fuss if we didn't let her know,' Jennifer began earnestly, and then faltered to a stop when Daniel threw her a look.

'Ring Mr Cooper's daughter, please, Jennifer,' he ordered firmly. 'I'll speak to her and she'll sort it out and tell her mother.'

He turned back to the patient as Jennifer bit her lip and hurried from the room. 'I've decided that another visit to hospital would be best, Joe. You need to see your specialist again and you've got too much pain to risk sending you home this time. We've got to see what's causing that back pain and I think you may have another kidney stone blocking up the works there.'

The man heaved a big sigh. Fear filled his eyes. 'Are

you sure? I don't want to go to hospital. They. . .' He closed his eyes.

'They do seem to rather like to keep you there, don't they?' Cindy said softly. She hesitated, and then added quietly, 'My father has the same disease as yourself so, believe me, I know what hospitals are like from the patient's point of view.'

She was aware of Daniel's head swinging sharply in her direction, but she smiled calmly at Joe and said cheerfully, 'But from what I've seen of this doctor he won't let that happen. If your tests are OK you'll probably be home before your wife's had time to miss you.'

Joe Cooper stared up at her for a long moment. Then Daniel moved to stand beside her. She felt his hand gently touch her shoulder as he gave a low chuckle. 'But his wife misses him if he even goes for a walk down to the sheds, doesn't she, Joe?'

A rather sheepish smile answered him. 'Yeah, she sure pressed the panic buttons that day, Doc.'

He saw Cindy's raised eyebrows and added rather drowsily, 'After the last spell in hospital, even at home the four walls closed in on me. Got the doc here out to look for me, she did, but by the time he arrived I was back having my morning cuppa.' He tried to move and pain twisted his face as he gasped, 'Doc here. . .likes. . . missus's cooking.'

He closed his eyes and did not see the relieved look that filled Daniel's face as they heard a vehicle pull up outside.

'Well, you'd only arrived home from hospital that morning, and your wife makes delicious scones,' Daniel said with a forced laugh. 'Now, I believe your ambulance has arrived, Joe, but I think I'll give you a little more for that pain. Where is it—still in the back?'

'Yeah,' the man gasped faintly.

Daniel's face was expressionless, but Cindy knew that

the pain probably meant that a vertebra had been damaged, possibly even given away, so that there was pressure on the spinal cord.

As he turned away to pick up the syringe he muttered rapidly to Cindy, 'BP elevated, pulse too fast, diminished urine output. Last blood test calcium was again on the increase. Andrew said he'd been trying to talk him into another bone marrow test, but he kept putting him off.'

Remaining where she was, she let Daniel see Joe off, and then stared after the procession out to the ambulance. Having quickly scanned his notes, she realised that although Joe Cooper had not been diagnosed as long as her father his disease seemed more advanced. He was thinner, paler and certainly had more pain.

Cindy clenched her teeth. Well, more pain than she had ever seen her father with, but it was highly probable that only her father and mother knew just how much pain he suffered. Always they had tried to protect their children, even those who had reached adulthood. And now. . .

She needed to be busy to battle her welling emotions. Grabbing her bag, she hurried out to the waiting room. Jennifer was tidying some magazines, and she said to her, 'I'm off to do the house call to Mrs Hoad.'

Before she had taken more than a couple of hasty steps Jennifer moved quickly and deliberately stood in front of her.

Cindy blinked rapidly, trying desperately not to let the tears stinging her eyes fall.

'Dr James, I need to speak to you,' the woman said so coldly that Cindy stiffened.

'Can't it wait, Jennifer?'

Jennifer hesitated and then said bluntly, 'No, I don't think it can, not after what I interrupted just before.'

Cindy stared at the woman in utter disbelief. She gritted her teeth, but managed to say calmly, 'I don't believe that my relationship with Daniel is any of your business, Jennifer.'

The receptionist gave a harsh laugh. 'No, it's not, but I thought I should warn you.'

Fighting for composure, Cindy raised an eyebrow and waited.

'There's already talk about you in the town. It doesn't take much to harm a doctor's reputation.' She gave a grim smile. 'I was very glad when at last you stopped living together. His mother was worried about you when I saw her a couple of times. She also heard about you two on the beach together. And I'm no fool.' Her voice rose. 'Don't kid yourself that I don't know what was going on in your room before.'

Cindy fought to hold onto her temper. If there was gossip about her and Daniel she knew who had started it!

Before she could find the right words to put this woman right the outside door where the ambulance picked up patients slammed shut.

Jennifer lowered her voice and hissed very quickly, 'You'll never get anywhere with him. He and his wife were very much in love, and that young daughter of his will do anything she can to stop her father marrying ever—'

Daniel strode into the waiting room, and she broke off and hurriedly bent and picked up another magazine from a chair.

Daniel obviously noticed the tension between them. He paused and glanced enquiringly from one to the other, and a twinkle filled his eyes as he raised an eyebrow at Cindy.

Suddenly Cindy couldn't bear any more. She turned away, tossing over her shoulder, 'I'm off to do a house call.' She strode off, pretending not to see the sudden frown Daniel gave her.

'I'll ring you later,' he called after her, but she just waved and kept going.

She was glad Mrs Hoad lived some distance out of town. Cindy gripped the steering-wheel tightly, forcing herself to concentrate on her driving despite the turmoil of thoughts and feeling that flooded through her.

Her first reaction had been of sheer anger at the receptionist's effrontery. By the time she had climbed into her car that had given way to deep pain.

That pain stayed with her while she dressed Mrs Hoad's ulcers. The old lady was even more talkative and full of the town's gossip than usual. Cindy listened to her with only half her attention until she mentioned the Nichols.

Then she raised her head sharply as Mrs Hoad said, 'Such a shame about that boy having auto. . .auto. . .that ism or something. I believe Dr Burston must be a very good doctor to have picked up that was what was wrong with the poor little chap.'

Cindy eyed her calmly. 'So you know the Nichols, do you, Mrs Hoad?'

'Me? No, no, I was just talking to—' She stopped and looked uncertainly at Cindy as she threw down the pair of forceps in her hand with unnecessary force.

'Let me guess, Mrs Hoad,' she said sharply. 'Jennifer Coats told the postman, who told you.'

'Well, er, yes. You see, I'm at the end of his run, like, and he often comes in for a cuppa. He's quite good friends with Jenny.'

Cindy thought carefully all the way home. Why was Jennifer so antagonistic towards herself, and should she tell Daniel her suspicions? Jennifer Coats had been working for the practice for some years. Surely in that time if she had been in the habit of breaching patient confidentiality Daniel's father would have found out? It was certainly grounds for instant dismissal! But how would they cope without her until Aileen was back at work?

Then she thought of what the woman had said about her and Daniel. Telling Daniel about that conversation would only be horribly embarrassing.

All the doubts Cindy had been battling since that first time he had kissed her had whelmed up again. If it was true that he had been wanting to kiss her, as he had claimed, it was not like the strong-minded, even at times arrogant man not to have done so.

And even if she had not been mistaken in interpreting his expression as love, was she prepared to be satisfied with being always the second best love of his life? Already his small daughter had crept into her heart, but could a relationship with her father ever survive her ongoing hostility to—apparently—any woman he loved?

She still had no answer when Daniel phoned her later that evening. Her heart did its usual gymnastics when she heard his deep, rich voice.

'Jennifer said you were upset. Are you OK now?'

'Yes, of course,' she answered stiffly.

There was silence for a moment, and then she heard the compassion in his voice as he said, 'I'm sorry about your dad, Cindy, love. Why didn't you tell me that day in the car when you were talking about your family?'

'I. . .I suppose over the years since he was diagnosed I've tried not to think about it too much. . .' Emotion choked her voice and she stopped.

'Oh, love,' he said softly, 'I can't leave Brittany, but would you like to come over here for a while?'

Yes, yes! Cindy wanted to shout at him, but mention of Brittany made her hesitate.

'I. . .I really think I need an early night,' she faltered instead.

'Oh.'

The disappointment in his voice was unmistakable, and impulsively she opened her mouth to say she'd changed her mind when he spoke again. 'That probably would be best, Cindy.' She nearly cried out at the distance in his voice, but it softened again as he said slowly, 'I know you're fine now, but I guess it has been a pretty emotionally charged day.'

Cindy swallowed, but before she could speak he whispered, 'Oh, Cindy, why do you have to be a doctor, too?'

Words froze in her throat.

'But we will get together and sort this out soon, won't we?' he said in a louder voice.

Was her being a doctor that big a problem for him? And what did he mean by 'this'? Was it the tenderness she had seen in his face? Was it the white-hot desire that had flared up between them, or what she had said about liking his family? Or. . .or that love she had thought she had seen so briefly. . .

He was certainly right. They had to talk.

Her grip on the receiver tightened. 'I. . . Yes. I. . . I'd like that,' she murmured back.

He gave a sigh and a low chuckle. 'And next time we'll make sure we don't have kids or receptionists anywhere in our vicinity.'

The phone went dead, and Cindy reluctantly hung up. A few moments later she realised she was still standing near the phone, staring into space. He had called her 'love'.

But why did he wish she was not a doctor? Because he wanted to have an affair with her and she worked for him? Or because. . . His wife had been a doctor. Did she in some way remind him too much of her? Or, with their heavy workload, had he decided that marriage between two doctors just did not work for him?

She moved abruptly. Here she was again, thinking about marriage when he had never even told her he loved her.

Cindy didn't sleep very well, and was tired before she

started the day. And once again it was a very hectic day from the word go.

Daniel was also running a little late and he returned her unexpectedly shy smile with a brief gleam of white teeth as they both raced past the already waiting patients to their respective rooms. He looked very weary, and Jennifer accusingly told her that Daniel had been called out during the night.

There were not usually very many night calls but, despite her protests, so far he had insisted she not be on call during the night.

'I don't think you know the outlying country tracks well enough yet,' he had insisted, but she had known he was still protecting her health, despite her insistence that she was now perfectly recovered.

Her lips firmed when she saw the black circles beneath his eyes when they met very briefly at lunchtime. It was about time she took her full share of the load now that his father had gone.

Unfortunately, he was rushing off to a call as she was ushering out her last patient. He smiled briefly at her again before he disappeared, leaving her feeling a sense of frustration at not having a chance to talk to him.

Her brother, Ben, had phoned her about John Nichols, and she had immediately wanted to tell Daniel all about it. Ben had confirmed their diagnosis, congratulating them on picking it up so early.

'Autism can be detected as early as thirty months but, unfortunately, is too often missed. The father is very badly shaken up but the mother seems almost relieved to be told there is actually something wrong.' He had sighed. 'I don't envy them. It's going to be a long, hard journey ahead for the whole family.'

The feeling of frustration at not having a chance to speak to Daniel had increased by teatime. There had been another busy afternoon at the surgery, which she had coped with alone while he was doing his house calls.

When she thought he should be home she had tried a couple of times to ring him, only to hang up hesitantly without leaving a message on his answering machine.

She tried one more time as the sun disappeared beyond the low hills west of Sandy cove.

The phone was answered by Brittany.

'Dr Burton's residence, Brittany speaking,' the young voice said efficiently.

Cindy had not seen Brittany since her Christmas play. She took a deep breath.

'Hello, Brittany, it's Cindy. Have you heard from your grandparents? Did they arrive safely?'

There was a brief silence, and then Brittany said a little too politely, 'Yes, thank you.'

'Is. . .is your dad there?'

Again that pause. 'No, he's not. Will that be all, Dr James?'

Cindy didn't smile at the little voice trying to sound grown-up and businesslike. There had been too much antagonism as well. She sighed inwardly. Apparently her hopes that the girl would be friendlier to her since the school concert had not been realised.

'When he comes in would you ask him to call me, please, Brittany?' she said crisply, and hung up.

She hesitated, annoyed with herself for letting the girl's abruptness get under her skin. It was very unusual for Brittany to be home by herself, and she wondered if the girl had been lying.

She shrugged. 'You're getting paranoid, Cindy James,' she muttered out loud. But her heart ached. What was it about her that the small girl disliked so much?

A little while later, just as she was thinking wearily of forcing herself to eat something, there was a knock on her door.

Daniel at last.

She rushed to the door with a quickened heart rate, only to stare with astonishment at the small girl thrusting out a rather bedraggled handful of daisies at her.

'Why. . .why, Brittany, thank you.' She stammered slightly as she took them from the scowling girl. A warm glow filled her and she beamed, but her brief pleasure quickly vanished.

'It wasn't my idea, it was Dad's.' There was scorn both in voice and glowering face. 'He said to also give you a message.' She hesitated and rattled off, 'He said to tell you these are for you and goodbye.'

Before Cindy could respond she had raced away.

Cindy's glow faded to disappointment and then astonishment, both at the message and. . .

Obviously someone had gone to considerable trouble to make the bouquet attractive with ribbon and wrapping paper, but the wrapping paper was torn and the once-beautiful, large white flowers were more than bedraggled, as though picked by a child. There were a couple of empty stems where the heads had been broken off and remaining petals were bruised and crushed.

By one dirty, small, angry foot?

Such wanton destruction of something that Daniel had seemingly tried to do to help her relationship with his daughter made her suddenly very angry. This young madam could do with a good spanking or telling-off at the very least, and what did she mean by that rude 'goodbye' business?

For a moment ice swept through her.

Was Daniel retreating from their new intimacy?

For a brief moment fear descended, but then she straightened. No way would the man she was getting to know use such a means to stop a blossoming relationship.

But she had to see him. She had to know. . .

Cindy raced into the bedroom and reached for her purse. Then she hesitated. Would getting Brittany into trouble solve anything or would it make the girl hate her even more?

Cindy thought deeply for a moment and then her lips twitched. As long as she could remember, her mother had tried to drill into them all to 'return good for evil and thus heap coals of fire on the enemy's head'.

Could it work this time?

Her lips tightened. One thing was sure that for any relationship with Daniel to come to fruition one pint-sized kid had to be sorted out.

That evening, as she prepared her evening meal and tried to relax in front of the television, she worked out what she would do.

On the way to the surgery the next morning she stopped and bought the nicest, largest thank-you card she could find for an eight-year-old girl, wrote a polite note about the kind thought behind the flowers and mentioned that now Naomi had gone home perhaps Brittany would like to go to the beach with her instead one afternoon. She addressed it to Brittany and slipped it into Daniel's letter-box.

She smiled breezily at Daniel when he arrived later at the surgery. 'Did Brittany get my thank-you note?'

He raised his chin and glared at her. Suddenly he was the angry, arrogant man she had first met and she froze.

'Your card in no way makes up for your rudeness and Brittany's disappointment. It will only upset her more,' he snapped and stormed past her.

Her rudeness and disappointment?

Cindy took a deep breath, and slowly counted to ten. Obviously Brittany had been twisting the facts again. She started towards Daniel's room, and stopped. They both had patients waiting, and sorting this out would take longer than a couple of moments, especially with Jennifer hovering curiously.

She turned and stormed into her own room.

Not only did the daughter need a good smacking, but the father could do with a good punch! Right on that arrogant, perfect nose!

CHAPTER NINE

ANGER kept Cindy going the rest of the morning. Jennifer eyed her warily and was all efficiency. Patients were attended to with an extra brightness—and extra care, if they had but known, as Cindy made sure the anger seething inside her did not affect her concentration.

She would have liked nothing better than a stand-up, nose-to-nose confrontation with the most maddening man she had ever encountered. One minute she was on cloud nine, sure he loved her, and the next he was staring at her as though she were a bad smell he would rather not have in his vicinity.

Why had he been so angry with *her*?

She should be angry at him for trusting a little girl to deliver his gift and his message.

Cindy had come very close to ringing him up immediately and asking him what the real message had been. There was no doubt in her mind that the these-are-for-you-goodbye routine had been another example of Brittany trying to cause mischief. Daniel was not the type of man to dismiss a budding relationship through his daughter, especially when he could not help but know that she was antagonistic towards Cindy.

But her gut feeling still was that causing Brittany to be reprimanded severely by her father would be the very worst thing she could do.

She had that afternoon off and, after trying to swallow a few mouthfuls of late lunch, tried to take her anger and confusion out on the badly neglected, small front garden of the flat.

There was quite a strong breeze, but as she worked in

the sun with the smell of the warm, moist earth her pain and distress gradually eased. That is, until she pulled away a heap of creeper and found a small daisy bush with one solitary, struggling daisy of the same variety as the sad ones she had bundled into her garbage can when she had arrived back from the surgery.

Extra carefully, she freed it to the healing caress of the sun's rays.

A solitary tear stole down her cheek. She sniffed and wiped it away impatiently with the back of her gardening glove. Over the years she had been given beautiful bouquets of roses by would-be admirers, but nothing had touched her so much as that home-wrapped posy of cottage garden daisies.

She had been so absorbed in her dismal thoughts that she had only vaguely been aware of the increased traffic in the street. Then a couple of excitedly chattering children made her rather wearily raise her head.

Cindy glanced at them briefly and went to return to her weeding when she heard one of them call out impatiently.

'Come on, hurry up, Brit!'

She glanced around sharply, at the same time wiping away a stream of tears that had started trickling down her face. Brittany was standing a few feet away, staring at her solemnly.

Slowly Cindy stood up, not taking her eyes from the small face which was so like Daniel's except for those startling blue eyes.

'You're crying,' the small girl said with a catch in her voice.

Cindy stared at her silently, and made no further attempt to stop the flow of tears. Coals of fire? So be it!

Brittany looked towards her friends, hesitated and took a couple of steps closer to Cindy. She looked down where Cindy had been working, and Cindy knew immediately when she spotted the half-opened white daisy.

Her eyes flew back to search Cindy's face.

Then her little bottom lip quivered, and she suddenly looked so miserable that Cindy felt all her anger fade away. All she wanted to do was catch her up, cuddle her and kiss her pain away. But if she so much as moved towards the small child she suspected she would take to her heels.

'People do cry when they've been hurt and are unhappy when someone's been unkind to them,' she said huskily instead, holding Brittany's gaze steadily.

A tide of red filled the small face. Brittany drooped her head and scuffled her sandal in the dirt on the footpath.

'Why'd you send me the card?'

The words were so soft that Cindy hardly heard them.

'Oh, you've seen it already, then?'

There was a slight nod. Cindy was silent. She felt relieved. From what Daniel had said she had not been sure.

She waited until Brittany at last raised her head. Her suspicion and fear made Cindy's heart go out to her.

'Because you are a lovely little girl, and I'd like nothing better than to be friends with you,' she said softly.

Shy pleasure briefly chased away the fear, but anger took its place. 'You only say that 'cause you wanna get in good with Dad!'

Cindy put her head on one side, as though considering that. 'Yes,' she said honestly at last, 'I do want to be friends with you because I want to be friends with your father as well, and it makes him sad when we don't get on together.'

Brittany opened her mouth, but Cindy held up her hand and said emphatically, 'But I've also seen the way you can be with your grandmother and your aunt, and I've been very jealous of them.'

Those dark blue eyes filled with astonishment. 'You've been jealous of *me*?'

Cindy pulled a face. 'Not very cool for a grown-up, is it?'

Brittany considered that for a moment, and then Cindy was delighted to see a slight grin twitch her lips.

'Did you mean that bit on the card about taking me to the beach?'

'I sure did! I hate going by myself, and I'd love you to come, too.'

'Could we go now?'

'Right this minute?'

To Cindy's dismay, the eager, excited look vanished. 'I s'pose you've got a patient to see,' she said glumly.

'Nope, it's my afternoon and evening off. Your father's been looking after all of them since lunchtime.'

Brittany looked puzzled. 'But don't you have books and paper stuff to do?'

Cindy chuckled. 'Not on your sweet life,' she said fervently. 'I like to forget about work at home as much as I can.'

But suddenly she was angry with Daniel. Obviously his daughter was used to him working all the time. How dared he not spend more time with his precious little girl? And then she sobered. Was it Sally that Brittany remembered being too busy?

'Think you can run home and be ready in, say, ten minutes?'

Brittany suddenly beamed at her. 'Sure can!' Then she giggled. 'But you'd better take longer and wash your face.'

When Cindy looked at herself in the mirror a few moments later she grimaced. The dirt on her gloves had mingled with the tears and her face was streaked with mud. So she did take longer than she expected to wash and change quickly into her own swimsuit and beach coat.

Then a phone call from Naomi delayed her further. When she hung up her heart was lighter.

Their father had actually just completed the course of chemotherapy, having started it without telling them a couple of weeks ago, and was already much better.

The other good news was not entirely unexpected. Ben had announced his engagement at last to the lovely Nikki, and they would both be home for Christmas. So the parents were adamant that Cindy should try and get home for Christmas in a few days time to have a triple celebration.

It was a good half-hour before Cindy stopped her car outside the old weather-board house. She sounded the hooter, and then remembered that she had forgotten to make sure Brittany would let Aileen know where she would be.

Alighting quickly, she ran lightheartedly up the path, and then stopped abruptly. Brittany was sitting hunched over on the top step.

'Brittany, did you remember to—? Why, whatever's the matter?'

Cindy's heart sank as she saw the anger and hostility again in the face Brittany raised towards her.

'I've changed my mind,' she said furiously. 'You don't really want to take me and I'm not going.'

'Brittany!' Cindy strode closer and put her hands on her hips. 'What's this all about? Of course I want to take you. I don't say things I don't mean.'

'Oh, yeah? Then why are you late? I've been waiting ages!'

Cindy gritted her teeth for a moment. She supposed thirty minutes would seem like a long time to a suspicious little girl. Well, she had known she couldn't win her over that easily, didn't she?

'I'm sorry I'm late,' she said steadily, and forced a little laugh. 'I'm afraid you were right about it taking me longer to get ready than I thought.' She pulled a face. 'I hadn't realised most of the garden was on me, and then Naomi rang.'

With a surge of relief Cindy saw some of the anger disappear, but Brittany remained stubbornly seated.

'Did she get home all right?'

'Yes, she's fine.' Cindy hesitated briefly and said quietly, 'We didn't tell anybody here because you were all so upset already about your Uncle Andrew, but our father has been sick and he was bad again. She rang to tell me he's not as sick this time as we had been told.'

Brittany stared at her for a moment, then scrambled very slowly to her feet. 'Oh.' Sadness filled her face. 'My mummy got sick and she died.'

Cindy felt her breath constrict. Very casually she said, 'Yes, I know, sweetheart. That was a bad time for you and your dad, wasn't it?'

The little face closed up again. 'Are we still going swimming, then?'

Cindy hid her disappointment. It was only the second time Brittany had ever mentioned her mother. She had hoped this might be an opportunity to assure her she need not fear she would ever try and replace her mother.

She caught herself. Goodness, here she was imagining being married to Daniel and he was hardly speaking to her!

A grin twitched her lips, and then spread into a full smile. It was partly at herself.

'Race you to the car,' she called, and took off, making sure the little girl won.

As they drove off she suddenly took her foot off the accelerator. 'Oh, did you let Aileen know where you'd be?' She was satisfied with the vigorous nod.

'Of course. Dad said he'd skin me alive if I

didn't always let her know where I was.'

It was another brilliant evening. The heat of the sun had waned but, despite the breeze, it was still warm enough for a swim as they ran up to the top of the sand-hill.

Cindy paused to catch her breath and yelled breathlessly, 'You win!'

'Slowcoach!' Brittany scoffed, and raced ahead.

Cindy followed a bit more slowly, picking her way carefully in the deep, soft sand. Once over the last rise of the sand-hills the south-easterly wind was much stronger. Eagerly she looked out across the deep blue ocean, and then she frowned.

As far as the eye could see there were white flecks on the choppy sea. Normally the surf at this end of the sweeping beach was sheltered and mild, but now the tide was in and angry breakers rolled in and curled over in rapid succession.

Cindy was a strong swimmer, but her expertise had been developed in suburban swimming pools. Only occasionally over the years had she been able to succumb to the lure of the sea. She had not been on a surfboard since her teens when her brothers had reluctantly let her tag along.

The lifesavers' safety zone flags were still out further up the beach, but there was no sign of anyone on duty. No one seemed to be swimming, and there were only a handful of keen surfers still out beyond the tumbling, foaming surf, waiting for the swell to toss up the right wave to ride until it spent itself or tossed them under its savagery.

Brittany was running towards the flags but entered the water near another flag that fluttered its message towards the sea.

Sudden alarm swept through Cindy.

'Brittany, wait!' she called urgently, and began to run.

The small girl looked towards her for a moment from the edge of the water, and then waded forward. By the time Cindy reached the spot she was already out of her depth and body-surfing on the spent, foaming waves near the shoreline.

When she stood up and shook her head she had been washed further away from the safe zone marked out by the red and yellow flags.

'Brittany, it's not safe!' Cindy called out and started wading towards her. Her voice was lost in the crash and roar of a wave.

She knew Brittany was like a fish in the water, but fear clenched its fist on Cindy as she watched the small girl dive under an approaching wall of tossing foam and water. To Cindy's utter relief, she let the next wave carry her back closer. The spent wave curled around Cindy's legs and she felt the strong tug of the outgoing tide.

'Brittany, it's too rough! Why don't we. . .go around to the inlet swimming hole?' she finished to herself as Brittany disappeared again under another wave.

The next time she bobbed up she was much further out. Cindy waved frantically at her, beckoning her to come in. Brittany stared at her for a moment. A stubborn scowl swept the beaming grin from the little face. She glared her defiance and deliberately turned away and started swimming along the water to catch another wave as it formed.

'Oh, no, Brittany,' Cindy muttered loudly. 'Now is *not* the time to treat me like the wicked witch.'

Angrily Cindy dived under the next wave and started wading after her. She knew it was useless—there was no way the child could hear her over the noise—but as she got closer she tried again. 'Brittany, it's too dangerous and the lifesavers aren't on duty,' she yelled at the top of her voice and waved towards the empty beach.

She saw Brittany look towards the shore. For a moment

she hesitated. Cindy saw fear fill the little face just before she took a deep breath and, to Cindy's utter relief, started swimming quickly towards her.

She disappeared again beneath a towering, breaking wave. Cindy turned her own back just in time to take the force of the breaking wave on her back. After it had rolled on she turned back and desperately looked for the small body.

Brittany was further away still and started swimming frantically again even as Cindy spotted her. Cindy's heart plummeted further as she realised that the small figure had made no headway.

The water was now up to Cindy's armpits. Still wading strongly forward, and with her eyes fastened on the small girl, Cindy did not see the wave that reared up and then slammed into her. It knocked her off her feet. Water roared over her and she came up coughing and spluttering and out of her depth.

Frantically she swept her wet hair out of her eyes and dog-paddled as she looked around for Brittany.

For one terrifying moment she couldn't see her. Then she caught a brief glimpse of her, further away still. She took a deep breath and started swimming strongly towards her. The strong undertow of the next wave building up sucked her forward. It passed her and she started swimming again. Surfacing, she looked around and realised that she had made absolutely no progress.

And suddenly she remembered what Naomi had said about dangerous rips on this beach. That solitary flag near where they had entered the water must have been the dangerous rip warning.

Sometimes strong surf shifted the sand so that there would be a deep channel where the current was very strong as the tide went out. The innocent-looking waves kept rushing as usual towards the shore but the water underneath surged out into the Pacific Ocean, sweeping all in its path with it. Every year hundreds of surfers on Australian beaches were trapped and had to be rescued.

Even strong swimmers got caught out. And little girls, no matter how well they. . .

'Brittany!'

Her scream of fear was drowned out by the roar of a wave.

A small dark head bobbed up briefly a long way out, well beyond the white water. Then it disappeared again as another swell formed. The undertow was ferocious.

With fear gripping her, Cindy suddenly knew that where Brittany had been it would have been even stronger. There was no way she could fight the ferocious surge of water. She could only surrender herself to it.

Daniel, oh, Daniel, her heart screamed, even as she gave herself up to the current and let it sweep her away while she battled to stay afloat. With a burst of thankfulness she realised it was narrowing the gap between her and the valiantly swimming little girl.

At last she started swimming frantically again towards where she had last seen Daniel's daughter, and at long last made some progress.

Ever afterwards the next few moments were only a memory of terror-stricken searching, of the surge of utter relief at last of finding and grabbing the terrified little girl tightly, of trying to battle a force too strong, and of trying to keep both of their heads out of reach of the choking blue water that tried to fill their mouths and lungs.

Sometimes in the months to come Cindy was to wake up from the recurring nightmare, crying out again as she gasped over and over, 'Don't fight it! Let it carry us. Keep your strength for staying afloat.'

Vaguely she knew that somehow super-strength had been given her to reach Brittany and to hold onto her as they were swept out, far beyond the tumbling line of breakers and into the blue rolling waters.

They were even beyond the row of surfers with their long boards. Afterwards she was told that a few had tried to reach them, but only one exhausted young man succeeded. For one horrible moment Cindy wondered if the long dark shape in the water was a shark, and sobbed with relief when the last swell subsided and tossed it closer and she saw him.

He was too breathless to speak, but after several attempts they managed to haul the small girl onto his long board and cling together as the swell took them further and further out.

Timeless moments later, as Cindy stared helplessly at Brittany's small, grey face, there was at last the roar of the lifesavers' surf-rescue boat. Strong hands pulled the three of them to safety.

Then there was only the still, lifeless form of the little girl Daniel loved so much. Cindy fought off the hands that tried to hold her back.

'I'm. . .doctor. . .' she gasped. 'You. . .get us to. . . shore. . .'

Then somehow she was extending the small face. She noted the blue lips, took as deep a breath as she could and then tried to force air into lungs filled with water.

Shock rocked her. Where there should have been only air it sounded like bubbles being blown through a bottle of water.

Another breath. More bubbles.

Before she could remove her own mouth the small body heaved slightly. Sea water trickled out but the lips were still blue.

'Breathe, Brittany!'

But she didn't. Cindy filled her own lungs again.

Another breath. Another.

This time, hope. A touch of pink on the lifeless lips.

Cindy rolled Brittany over. The small body convulsed and water and sand shot out.

This time Brittany spluttered and choked, but started breathing by herself. At long last Cindy let others take over.

By the time the boat was being grabbed by eager hands and being hauled up the beach Brittany had got rid of most of the sea water in her lungs and stomach and lay clinging tightly to Cindy, crying softly.

Then there were strong hands trying to separate them, carrying them from the boat.

And Daniel.

A furious, horrified Daniel.

Cindy saw him grasp hold of his daughter. He glared at Cindy with such anger that she closed her eyes against his rage and at last drifted off into the grey haze that had been trying to close around her.

She woke up slowly, and gradually realised she was on a narrow hospital couch in an emergency room.

Cindy closed her eyes again thankfully, but they flew open almost immediately. A tearful small voice was swearing. Then it stopped, and short, stifled sobs disturbed her peace instead.

Then the swearing started up again. 'Damn, damn, damn Daddy!' Then there followed another word a lot worse!

Cindy started to roll over towards the sound, and pain jabbed through her. She groaned. At least it stopped the swearing.

'Cindy?'

'Brittany?' Goodness, was that croaky voice hers?

'You're. . .you're not dead?'

Cindy cautiously pulled herself up on one elbow and peered across at the other bed. This time only over-used muscles protested.

Brittany was sitting up, staring anxiously at her from a tear-streaked face.

'Well, if I'm dead you must be, too, Brittany Burston,' she managed with a grin.

Suddenly she was enveloped by a quivering, crying bundle of small girl. She held her tightly, closing her eyes and silently offering up a fervent prayer of thanks.

'I. . .I thought we were drowned.'

Cindy gave a weak chuckle. 'Nope, not us, sweetheart.'

Gradually the crying stopped as they clutched each other. At last Brittany pulled back. They studied each other's wet, pale faces. Someone had removed their swimming costumes and they were both in hospital gowns.

Cindy felt tears fill her eyes, realising just how much she loved this sturdy, brave little scrap.

Trying to stop her emotions upsetting Brittany again, she said with mock severity, 'Someone swearing horrible words woke me up. That wouldn't have been you by any chance, Brittany Burston?'

Rebellion flashed into the tear-drenched eyes, but before she spoke Cindy suddenly remembered.

'Daniel?' she said urgently, looking around the small room. 'Where's your father?'

Brittany gave a long sniff and then scowled. 'Oh, him?' she said crossly. 'He said he just had to go and ring Auntie Aileen before she heard some mixed-up story about us being dead.'

A shiver swept through Cindy and she shut her eyes tightly. It had been close. She hoped Brittany never realised just how close.

'Oh, Cindy,' Brittany wailed suddenly, 'he's awful mad at us.'

Cindy felt, in all fairness, she could hardly blame him!

But the terror was back in Brittany's eyes and Cindy

felt the shudders she was valiantly trying to control. Diversion was needed.

'Where on earth did you learn all those swear words, young lady?'

The fright faded. Brittany scowled at her. Cindy managed to scowl right back, instead of kissing and hugging her senseless.

After a long moment Brittany hung her head. 'One of the boys at school in Sydney was always getting into trouble for saying naughty words.' She gave a loud sniff. 'I was just so angry with Daddy!'

'Yeah, I get angry with him myself!' Cindy muttered. The drenched blue eyes widened, and she added hurriedly, 'Hmm, well, that's no excuse! Those words are far too horrible for a nice little girl like you to have pass her lips.'

Cindy had tried to sound as stern as she could but then she wrecked it anyway by hugging the little body closer.

She had taken this precious little girl, this precious daughter of the man she loved quite desperately, out to the beach and almost let her drown.

Sudden horror spread through her at their narrow escape. She started to shiver violently, and fought desperately not to burst into frightened tears herself. The room swayed around her again.

'Brittany!' a voice roared. 'I thought I told you in no circumstances were you to leave that couch!'

They both jumped, and Brittany gave Cindy such a resigned, old-fashioned look and shrug that, despite the shock coursing through her, she almost laughed out loud.

Almost.

They turned simultaneously towards the door, and all desire Cindy had to even smile vanished.

This was a Daniel she had never dreamed could exist.

His face was dead white, his eyes blazing. He was still wearing the clothes he had worn that morning, but the shirt and dark trousers were soaking wet and clinging to him—covered in sand and even a couple of pieces of seaweed. His tie was still half done up, but hanging miserably in a ruined mess.

'You're all wet,' Cindy muttered.

He ignored her. In two strides he reached them and plucked Brittany away from Cindy's arms.

'I told you not to disturb Cindy!' he exclaimed in only a slightly lower voice.

To Cindy's envy, as well as admiration, Brittany clasped him around the neck and strategically burst into tears again.

'Oh, please leave her, Daniel. I'm fine,' Cindy croaked hoarsely.

'You're nothing of the sort,' he rasped accusingly.

She shrank back and watched helplessly as he strode from the room, with Brittany clinging to him. He roared something outside. She thought it was something about seeing to that woman, but she was shaking more and more and then she, too, burst into tears, longing to feel his arms around her.

A nurse Cindy had met on a visit to the hospital bustled in. 'Truly! That man! We do have other patients worse than—' she started angrily, and then broke off and became the professional, calming person she usually was.

An extra blanket was quickly wrapped tightly around Cindy. A towel was produced and her hair rubbed dry.

When she stopped fussing Cindy had dried her eyes and, except for her hoarse voice and the cough that shook her occasionally, began to feel much better.

Some time later, after waiting alone for what seemed like aeons, she impatiently told the young hospital doctor who rushed in to examine her that she was 'fine, just fine'.

He muttered, 'That's good.' But he gave her a thorough examination, anyway, and ordered a chest X-ray, despite her protests. He muttered again something about keeping her in hospital overnight, and flew out again before she could voice a strong protest and question him about Brittany.

She was more than ready for Daniel the next time she saw him.

'I am definitely not staying in this hospital! I had enough of being a patient when I had pneumonia!' she tried to yell at him, and then burst into tears all over again.

Suddenly her quivering body was being cradled tightly in strong arms that shook slightly. He rocked her, murmuring soothing words until they were both calmer. As she at last rested against him quietly she realised his own trembling had stopped, too, and suddenly wondered who had been comforting who.

'I'm so sorry, Daniel—'

He moved his arms away so fast she fell back, gasping on a stab of pain as she hit the pillow and stared up at him.

His jaw was tight and his knuckles white as he raised a clenched fist and hit the side of the mattress. She couldn't bear the sudden agony that twisted his face.

'And so you should be!'

He swallowed convulsively and she couldn't find a word to say.

'I don't want to talk about it now,' he croaked at last in a harsh voice, and turned away.

He, too, was now wearing hospital clothes, but she could see the strong muscles beneath his gown ripple and she knew he was fighting for control.

Bewildered, she shrank back on the bed. Did he blame her even more than she blamed herself?

Misery lashed her.

The young doctor bustled back into the room but paused when he saw Daniel.

'Dr Burston, your daughter's demanding to be brought

back here,' he snapped angrily and, despite her confusion and pain, Cindy was amused.

The Burston father and daughter were definitely not in favour. Brittany must be giving the staff hell.

'Both your daughter's and Dr James's chests seem clear,' the doctor reeled off rapidly. 'Routinely we must keep them in hospital for observation for twenty-four hours. Besides shock, sometimes water might have passed from the lungs into the blood and the lining of the lungs may be damaged. This could be a life threatening—'

Daniel stopped him with one short, sharp, very loud word.

'Daniel!' gasped Cindy. 'Well, really, no wonder Brittany knows so many swear words!'

He flung around and impaled her with a glance. She glared right back. Suddenly she decided she had put up with enough.

She lifted her chin. Turning to the now rather flushed young doctor, she said strongly, 'We are both doctors, and probably know more than you about possible complications from near drowning, without you spelling it out so clearly at this precise moment.'

Her glance softened as it returned to the still grey-faced Daniel. 'And you forgot to mention the shock which relatives and rescuers often suffer from almost equally with victims!'

She swung her legs over the bed and stood up. It was too ambitious and she felt her body sway. Both men took a quick step towards her.

Cindy flopped back onto the side of the bed and waved them back imperiously. She closed her eyes, fought the wave of dizziness, and then glared up at them both.

With all the command she could muster, she snarled, 'Andrew should be home. That makes two doctors to care for us. I'm going home. And, somehow, I'm sure

Brittany will be better off there, too. She's been upset enough'

She took a deep breath.

'Now, are you going to help me, Daniel? Or do I have to walk out of here and get someone else to drive me?'

CHAPTER TEN

OF COURSE, it was not as easy as that.

The hospital doctor point-blank refused to allow them to take Brittany home for at least another couple of hours, and because Cindy did know the risks after a near drowning she acquiesced reluctantly.

Brittany was reinstated next to her in the curtained-off cubicles. As a grim-faced Daniel gently lowered her onto the couch she grinned triumphantly across at Cindy and promptly fell asleep. Cindy closed her eyes, but only managed to doze lightly, jolting awake frequently to anxiously check that Brittany was still resting quietly, still breathing.

Each time the dishevelled, grim figure of Daniel was still slumped in a chair, watching them both. The first time she caught his dark gaze her heart contracted, waiting for him to approach her.

For a few moments they stared at each other. His face was in the shadows and she could not read his expression as the tension built up between them. She longed intensely for him to hold her again, to make her feel safe. Abruptly he broke their eye contact. With a quick turn of his head he stared again at his daughter.

Defeated for the moment and close to tears again, she let her head fall back on her pillow. He was still too furious even to talk to her.

At long last, despite her breaking heart, Cindy did allow the exhaustion and analgesia she had been given to overwhelm her and she slept. She woke once again to Brittany's loud, irritable voice.

'I don't *want* to stay in this stupid hospital. I want to go *home*!'

As Cindy tried to wake up properly she heard Daniel's urgent whispers trying to quieten her. His stubborn daughter was not to be placated.

'But the nurse told me Cindy doesn't want to stay here either. *Please*, Daddy!'

Cindy knew it was time to let them both know she was awake. 'You are perfectly right, Brittany. I want to go home too,' she said loudly.

There was silence. Then Daniel's exasperated voice said loudly, 'Now look what you've done, young lady. You've woken up Cindy.'

'Good,' snarled his 'young lady' viciously and *very* loudly. 'Perhaps now we can get outta this horrible place!'

Cindy painfully swung herself up and sat on the side of the couch. 'How is she?' she asked Daniel's unfriendly back. She stared at him hungrily and saw the muscles across those massive shoulders flex and stiffen. Very slowly he turned around and impaled her with his eyes as they searched her face.

Before he could speak Brittany slipped off the couch behind him and flew across the room towards Cindy.

'Oh, Cindy, make him tell that other doctor to let us go home!' the little girl wailed.

Daniel's face contorted angrily and he took a hasty step to try and grab Brittany, but she successfully dodged him and scrambled up beside Cindy. She automatically put her arm around the small body that snuggled up to her, trying not to wince as her shoulder muscles protested.

'You both look so pale. I. . .I. . .' He stopped and swallowed convulsively, and then his face lightened slightly with relief as the young doctor swept aside the cubicle curtains.

Cindy looked down at the tear-dampened blue eyes

turned pleadingly up to her. Brittany was pale, but Cindy wholeheartedly believed they would both be able to recover better at home. She winked at her, and was delighted when Brittany gave her a slightly trembly smile but winked right back. She took a deep breath, and together they turned to do battle with the doctor.

It took a while. The doctor wanted to do more tests, still insisting on sticking to the hospital routine of twenty-four hours admission. Only once did Cindy glance at Daniel for support. He merely tightened his lips, glowered back at her and said nothing.

'If you don't let me go home I'll yell and keep *everybody* awake,' Brittany exploded at last to the by now angry young doctor. She gave a huge sob and screamed again, 'I want to go *home*!'

At last the doctor threw up his hands in defeat. He snapped out a few terse instructions to the attending, suitably grave-faced nurse and stormed out of the room. A slight grin crept across the nurse's face before she controlled herself and hurried off to obey his instructions.

Cindy glanced triumphantly at the silent, arms-crossed Daniel. She thought she saw a fleeting look of relief ease the stern look on his face, but he merely scowled back when he saw her watching him.

Cindy quickly discovered she was still very shaky, and very reluctantly she allowed a nurse to take her out to Daniel's car in a wheelchair, while he strode beside them with his now very subdued little daughter tightly in his arms.

After carefully putting Brittany onto the passenger seat beside him, he returned to help settle Cindy into the back. His strong jaw was tense, and he still looked like a man hanging onto his self-control by a thread.

Cindy's muscles screamed when she tried to put on the seat belt. His strong hands took over, brushing lightly against her breast as he reached across her. She stiffened and he took his hands away as though stung.

The sun had long since set, and for one long moment they stared at each other in the dim light filtering through the car. For one heavenly moment she thought he moved closer, as though to kiss her, but then torment darkened his eyes until they seemed almost black. He drew back, slammed the car door and strode around to the driver's seat.

The guilt and despair which had been settling more and more on her at the hospital swept through her with numbing, tongue-tying effect.

She doubted whether he would ever be able to forget or forgive her gross stupidity. She found it hard to forgive herself, knowing she deserved everything he thought about her.

Not once had she considered the strength of the south-easterly wind that had been blowing all that day. She should have known that it would transform that usually fun parlour of ocean into a seething, heaving mass of potential destruction.

Even the overworked lifesavers had apparently gone off duty early when the beach had been practically deserted all afternoon except by the few hardy, very experienced surfers.

Brittany had lived there too short a time to have been taught respect for the treachery of the surf, but long enough to have become a little too self-confident.

Brittany quickly went to sleep again, but for Cindy the long trip home was agony, both physically and emotionally.

By the time the silent, grim-faced Daniel drove the car past the WELCOME TO SANDY COVE sign on the town's outskirts Cindy was wishing fervently she had not been so stubborn and been a good little patient and stayed in hospital like the good big doctor had insisted! Her head was throbbing viciously, and she felt as though every muscle in her body had been battered into a painful mess.

Cindy felt so miserable and exhausted when Daniel pulled into the drive at his house and not her flat that she made no protest. Neither did she dare look at him when he growled, 'Don't move. I'll be back for you.' He disappeared into the house with Brittany.

Then he was back, helping her out of the car. Her head gave a sharp throb and she winced as she tried to take a step supported by his strong arm. Sore muscles cramped and she gave a low, barely stifled moan that had him sweeping her up into his arms.

But as he strode into the house and at last into a bedroom there was no sense of intimacy in his clasp. He was as austere and impersonal as any man might be with a perfect stranger.

Weak tears began streaming down Cindy's face as he placed her carefully on a bed. To her utter dismay he ignored her distress.

Daniel straightened and walked out of the bedroom. She had longed for him to comfort her, as he had at the hospital, and she felt utterly bereft.

The tears fell faster, but suddenly Aileen was there.

'Oh, Cindy, you poor, brave darling,' she soothed. 'Do you think you could sit on a chair under the shower? Daniel said a hot bath would be better, but he thinks you're too exhausted. You'd feel a lot better if you let hot water relax those muscles.'

She did feel better just getting rid of the salt and sand, but the hot water did little for the pain in the over-used muscles or the pain in her heart. She collapsed gratefully back into bed in one of Daniel's mother's nightgowns.

Aileen left a small lamp on, before hurrying away. A few minutes later Cindy heard a movement in the room and opened her eyes to see Daniel, studying her.

'Daniel, I'm. . . I'm. . .' she began urgently, desperate

to tell him again how sorry she was, and that she was quite prepared to even leave the practice for somewhere else if he could not forgive her.

He put a finger to his lips. 'Not now, Cindy, not now,' he said huskily.

Relief swept through her that he no longer sounded angry.

'I've brought you another painkiller and a sleeping tablet,' he continued quietly. 'You've had more than enough for one day. We'll talk some other time.'

She stared back at him helplessly, knowing he was right.

'No sleeping tablet,' she said faintly at last.

He hesitated, then nodded abruptly. She let him raise her head so she could swallow the tablets, savouring the firm strength in his arms. He turned away the moment she had finished.

'Daniel, is Brittany. . .? Is Brittany really all right?'

She watched his tall figure stiffen, before slowly turning back to face her.

'She's fine, Cindy,' he said in such a shaky voice that it shook her more than anything else he had said to her. 'A little shocked still and sore but, thanks to you, she's fine.' His voice was rough with reigned-in emotion.

She heard him clear his throat, before adding quickly, 'I have to go back to her. She's waiting for me.'

The moment his disturbing presence was gone she longed for him to come back with an intensity she had not dreamed was possible. But what was there for them to talk about? At least he seemed to give some credit to her for saving Brittany's life, but he was obviously finding it very hard to forgive her for her stupidity in leading her into danger in the first place.

It seemed a long time before the painkillers worked and she could at last succumb to the exhaustion that swept her into a deep, healing sleep.

Only once did she stir. A deep voice hushed her gently, and she realised she must have been calling out in her sleep. A gentle hand smoothed back her hair from her hot forehead and stroked her cheek. With a deep sigh she relaxed again, and the next time she woke the sun was high in the morning sky.

Despite what she had hoped, as soon as she tried to get out of bed Cindy knew there was no way she was well enough to work that day. Her overstretched muscles protested vigorously, and she was surprised at how exhausted she felt.

She knew she had no choice but to obey the orders Daniel had left with Aileen to rest. But she did firmly refuse his instructions to stay in bed.

Fortunately, as Aileen explained, she had brought Andrew home the day before, and he was quite capable of minding their two while she popped in and out to keep an eye on Brittany and Cindy.

Christmas was only two days away but Cindy noticed with some surprise that there were only a very few decorations throughout the house. Seeking anything to brighten up Brittany's pale little face, Cindy queried Aileen.

She looked concerned for a moment and then sighed. 'I guess there just hasn't been enough hours in the day for my brother to even think of Christmas yet.'

She quickly dragged out her mother's artificial Christmas tree and decorations, and with a laugh left Brittany and Cindy exclaiming over discovered treasures.

Making sure neither of them became too tired, Cindy organised the decorating of Daniel's abode, hoping he would not add this impertinence to his other list of her misdemeanours.

But Cindy only saw Daniel briefly when he checked on them at lunchtime. He took in the sparkling little tree and the decorations in the lounge room with one sweeping glance. A brief frown touched his face and then it softened. He gave his daughter a quick hug and dutifully admired their efforts, all without looking directly at Cindy.

Before she could say a word about wanting to speak to him he hurriedly said he had a mountain of house calls and paperwork to do and rushed out again.

Cindy's already heavy heart sank lower. He was still avoiding any confrontation with her. Whether his withdrawal was because he did not trust his temper or because he wanted to wait until she had recovered enough to receive a full blast, she wasn't quite sure. One thing she grimly became determined on as the day passed was that there would have to be some kind of confrontation—and soon!

Brittany seemed to lap up all the attention from Cindy and her aunt. Despite still looking rather pale, the small girl had recovered much faster than Cindy. And what was like considerable balm to Cindy's sore heart—Brittany had completely changed her attitude towards her, hardly letting her out of her sight.

Obviously to at least one small girl she had obtained heroine status!

'You'll have to go swimming a lot more, Cindy,' Brittany told her firmly after lunch as she watched Cindy moving stiffly away from the table, 'then your muscles wouldn't be so sore.'

Cindy shuddered inwardly, but merely smiled as the girl curled up on the lounge beside her. She thought it would be a long, long time before she would swim in the ocean again!

'Cindy, I'm sorry I've been so mean to you.' Brittany's voice was very soft.

Cindy gave her an extra hug. 'That's all right, sweetheart. I can understand that you don't want to share your dad with anyone else.'

Brittany jerked upright. 'Share Dad? What do you mean?'

Cindy stared at the puzzled little face. 'Sometimes when a child loses one of her parents she can be afraid of losing the other one, too, even if it's by his close attention to another person,' she said very carefully. 'And. . .' Cindy took a deep breath '. . .resent the possibility of him marrying someone else.'

Brittany stared up at her and big tears slowly filled her eyes and spilled over.

Cindy hauled her into her arms. 'Oh, Brittany, don't cry! I. . .' She stopped. It was too, too painful to put her shattered dreams into words, but she had to face reality. 'I did think your dad might be starting to like me. . .like me a lot. But now he. . .he's very angry with me and doesn't like me at all.'

Brittany shook her head vigorously. Cindy let her go and a small hand scrubbed furiously at the tears.

'He does like you. He likes you lots and lots. He watches you all the time with a real soppy look. And he kissed you!'

Cindy's heart leapt. She had been right. It had even been obvious to a child. Daniel had been falling in love with her. And then her heart sank again. *Had* was the right word.

Brittany's confession rushed on. 'That. . .that's why I was mean to you. If he liked you enough to make you my new mother, like Jennifer said, then he'd *never* tell me ever about my real mum. And then I got even more scared because I liked you so much. You'd be a great mother!' she wailed.

Cindy gave a startled, 'Oh, Brittany!' But the trembling voice rose and kept pouring out all the confusion and hurt that had apparently been building up ever since the receptionist in Sydney had asked Brittany if she would mind if one day her father asked her to be the girl's new mother.

'But I told Daddy, and he was very angry and said there had never been any chance of that, and that he never wanted to ever be married again, and then we left earlier than he'd been planning and came here.'

Brittany gave a big sob that shook Cindy even more than her words.

'But then you came, and he kissed you, and I was scared again. And then when he sent me over to give you the flowers to show I was really, really sorry for telling lies and to ask you to tea I met Jennifer as she was leaving the centre and she. . .Jennifer said how pretty the flowers were and I told her they were for you.

'She. . .she laughed all funny, and then told me he was probably going to ask you to be my mother and it would help me to forget my real mother. I. . . I. . .'

This time the tears developed into heartrending sobs and she wailed, 'I don't want to forget my mummy! Sometimes I already can't remember what she even looks like. I'm so scared I'll forget her altogether. So I was so angry I jumped all over the flowers, and didn't ask you to come.

'And then I told Daddy you were cross and said you didn't want to eat with a horrible kid like me, and I cried and cried because I'd told him a big, *big* lie and. . .and I keep hoping and hoping he'll tell me about my mum, but Daddy never talks about her and when she died he cried and cried! He looks so sad and upset when anybody talks about her I couldn't ask him to. I don't want him to be sad!'

Cindy stared at the small, tormented face. Daniel had forbidden her to speak to his daughter about her mother because she got upset, but all the time she had been longing desperately to talk about her mother so she would not forget her!

The foolish, foolish man! Both father and daughter had been denied the privilege of comforting each other by talking together about the wife and mother they had both loved and lost.

She managed to soothe Brittany and at last asked her to tell her what she could remember about Sally Burston. The more she falteringly talked about her mother, the more Brittany seemed to remember. But, to Cindy's way of thinking, it was still pitifully little. She could not remember any picnics together or even a favourite book her mother had read to her.

Once again she remembered what Daniel had said and suddenly wondered just how much time Sally had spent with her daughter. It seemed very little for a then-five-year-old to have so few precious memories.

At last Cindy said slowly, 'Brittany, I want you to promise me something.'

Brittany looked at her solemnly and then nodded.

'I want you to ask your father to tell you all about your mother.' Fear filled the rounded eyes and Cindy said quickly, 'He hasn't wanted to talk to you about her because he thought it would only upset *you*.'

She smiled lovingly at the sudden glint of wonder in Brittany's face. 'You've both been a pair of dills, don't you think?'

Daniel did not arrive home again until teatime. But there was no chance to talk to him, to tell him about her conversation with Brittany. He looked absolutely exhausted, swallowed very little food and barely said half a dozen words to any of them before he rushed off to take the evening surgery—surgery that should have been Cindy's.

His obvious lack of appetite had equalled her own and Cindy felt even more guilty at the extra work that he was once more forced to do. She remembered his presence in her room during the night, and suddenly wondered if he had slept at all, or had kept vigil over her and his daughter.

But, above all, she was desperately hurt by his continuing grim attitude towards her. Why, he had hardly glanced at her the whole time he was in the house!

Then her hurt turned to anger with him and, despite Aileen and Brittany's protests, she insisted on returning to her own flat to sleep.

But by the time she had given up any hope that Daniel would call and see her that night she was feeling so lonely and wretched that she wished, once again, that she had not been so stubborn. Had she stayed at his house, she would have at least had some chance of speaking to him, no matter how late he finished work.

It was very late before she gave up, dosed herself with more painkillers and went to bed.

CHAPTER ELEVEN

BY THE next morning, except for a few stiff muscles, Cindy felt much better. However, when she presented herself at Jennifer's desk for her list of patients for the morning surgery the woman gaped at her.

'Dr James! I. . . We. . .didn't expect you to work today,' Jennifer stammered.

Cindy raised an eyebrow. 'I'm fine,' she said shortly.

The receptionist looked at her haughtily and said officiously, 'But Daniel said—'

She broke off. Cindy was furious. She had drawn herself up and thrust out her hand for the charts. She glared at the woman, in no mood for any petty nonsense.

'My charts, please, Jennifer.'

Jennifer hesitated for a moment and then handed a couple to Cindy.

'Only two?'

'Daniel took the others. I was just trying to phone these two patients to alter their appointments.'

Cindy glanced at the patients' names. 'Right,' she said briskly, 'there's no need now, is there? And I'll see Dr Burston myself,' she added grimly, and stormed off to confront Daniel.

Perhaps it was fortunate that he had started early and already had a patient with him. In fact, it was one of her patients that had been scheduled today to have sutures removed, one of the cut-glass casualties.

Cindy forced a smile and nodded to both of them, ignoring the rather startled expression on Daniel's face.

'Good morning, gentlemen. I've just come for my other charts, Dr Burston.'

She was the recipient again of one of Dr Burston's famous scowls, but as he opened his mouth the young man on the examination couch exclaimed, 'Dr James! Wasn't it you who rescued that little girl yesterday?'

With surprise and then compassion, Cindy noticed Daniel's face lose all its colour.

Before either of them could speak the patient rushed on, 'Man, you were great! They said she wouldn't have made it but for you.'

She stiffened, managing with difficulty to push back the sudden memory of dark, heaving water. Somehow she forced a smile, something she seemed to have had to do quite a lot lately. 'Not true,' she said as steadily as she could. 'Neither of us would have made it but for a very brave young man and his surfboard and the speed of the lifesavers.'

The kidney tray in Daniel's hand rattled sharply. He thumped it down on the tray. Cindy glanced apprehensively at him but his suddenly pale face was a professional mask.

Cindy moved towards the desk quickly and sorted through the pile of charts. She picked up a few and looked up defiantly at Daniel.

'Mine, I believe,' she said sweetly.

She did not wait for his response, before turning and marching out. When she reached her own examination room she found she was trembling, and wasn't quite sure why. Was it because of the reminder of the accident—or the bleak, defeated look that had entered Daniel's face as she had turned away?

Cindy coped very well with the stream of patients that morning. Then the teenager she had seen her very first day and suspected of having an eating disorder arrived.

Carefully schooling her face not to show her shock at the girl's thin figure, Cindy immediately asked the worried-looking woman accompanying her if she minded staying in the waiting room until she had finished examining her daughter.

The woman drew herself up autocratically. 'I want to stay with my daughter, Dr James,' she said firmly, at the same time pushing past Cindy in the doorway.

Cindy was tired and felt less like insisting than she ever had. She had always respected a mother's right to hear what was said and done to her child, even when that child was a young teenager, but this woman had been impossible the last time. There was no way this fifteen-year-old would open up to her if her domineering mother stayed.

She remained near the open door and said to the girl, 'Do you really want your mother to stay and hear our discussion, Amanda?'

The girl looked up at her with a defiant glare. 'I couldn't care less what she does,' she snapped.

Cindy returned her look steadily, and then raised her eyebrows warningly. 'Are you quite, quite sure about that?' she asked very quietly.

The girl stared at her for a moment and then looked scared. She turned towards her mother. 'Oh, Mum, you'd better wait outside, I suppose,' she said with a shrug of indifference that in no way fooled Cindy.

The woman blustered and fumed, but Cindy held the door open and at last ushered her out.

Cindy had hardly taken her seat before the girl said in a rather shrill voice, 'I suppose you're going to ask me all about my sex life and all that stuff.'

'Do you think that's what I should do, Amanda?' Cindy asked quietly.

The girl glared at her for a moment and then dropped her eyes and muttered, 'Do. . .do you think I might have AIDS?'

Cindy picked up her pen and studied it for a moment as she twirled it between her fingers. At last she said softly, 'Am I to infer from that there is some reason to be afraid you may have contracted AIDS? Are you sexually active?'

The girl lifted her head and shrugged with some bravado. 'Of course I've been having sex,' she said scornfully. 'Who hasn't?'

Me, for one, Cindy could have told her—and you, Amanda, my dear, are under-age.

The girl added quickly, 'But only safe sex, of course.'

And how many babies have been conceived by people using condoms as 'safe sex', Cindy also nearly told her grimly.

Instead, she straightened and said briskly, 'Sensible girl. Now, why did you mention AIDS at all then?'

A flash of fear again swept across the girl's face. 'There was a programme on the telly about AIDS in Africa. They call it the "wasting disease" there.' She paused and then blurted out fearfully, 'A friend of mine told me I was starting to look just like some of them on that show. That's why I let Mum talk me into coming to see you again.'

Very carefully, Cindy said, 'We can certainly do some blood tests, if you're worried about it, but there's also another disease in our civilisation that could make you very thin, Amanda, especially among teenage girls. Have you read up on anything about it?'

The girl scowled angrily again. 'Thin? I'm not too thin. Mum's just a real worry wart.'

'Ever heard of anorexia?' Cindy asked bluntly.

The girl hesitated for a moment and then gave a slight nod, avoiding looking at Cindy.

'Over thirty-seven women and girls suffering from this eating disorder were hospitalised in the Hunter area during the last twelve months, and the experts believe that's only the tip of the iceberg,' Cindy continued crisply.

Amanda did look at her then, even though her face was filled with defiance.

Holding her gaze steadily, Cindy added quietly, 'It has been reported that in one year more than 240 patients out of 1,243 sufferers of anorexia and bulimia admitted to New South Wales hospitals died.' She paused for effect, knowing she could have added that undoubtedly some of those deaths would have been suicides directly related to the condition.

But she merely added softly, 'By far the majority were aged between fifteen and twenty.'

Good. At last Amanda was starting to look apprehensive.

Cindy stood up. 'Right. Step on these scales please, Amanda,' she instructed in her best no-nonsense voice.

As she had thought, the girl had lost several more kilograms, but she only smiled proudly when Cindy pointed it out.

Cindy sighed. This poor girl was in for a long, long haul both to hospital and psychiatric treatment.

It took some time, but gradually Cindy managed to get the girl to tell her about the way she only pretended to eat, and the time when she was forced to do so about the laxatives she dosed herself with and the self-inflicted vomiting.

By the time she had enough facts to present to the slightly subdued, even more worried mother and they had both persuaded Amanda to be admitted to hospital, Cindy was exhausted.

She was immensely relieved when the woman finally stood up to leave, promising to take her daughter straight to the hospital. But after the woman had almost pushed her reluctant daughter out of the room she rounded on Cindy.

'You still had no right to stop me being here while you talked to Amanda, Dr James. After all, you are only a trainee doctor. Jennifer agrees with me, and I'm going to complain to your superior about your attitude!'

Her superior? A trainee?

Cindy stared blankly at the door after it had clicked sharply closed behind the woman. Now where on earth did this woman get to think. . .?

Technically speaking, she supposed Daniel was her superior, but she was certainly not a trainee as such. She had been a fully qualified doctor now for nearly four years, with only a few more months before she could register as a general practitioner. Besides, how many patients would even know she was doing her GP training?

The obvious answer tightened her lips and sent her striding out to the waiting room. It was empty, and Jennifer was not behind her counter. She was busy ushering Amanda and her mother out at the front door.

It gave Cindy time to take a grip on her temper and consider carefully what she should say to the receptionist who had been trying to undermine her so many times in the last few weeks.

Jennifer re-entered the waiting room and stopped when she saw Cindy.

'Come into my room, Jennifer,' Cindy ordered abruptly and turned away, but the receptionist did not move. 'Or we can discuss this right here and now,' she snapped.

Jennifer glared at her belligerently. 'Discuss what?'

Cindy took a step closer. 'Why you are so unpleasant to me, why you have tried to make sure Brittany doesn't like me, and. . .' anger made her raise her voice '. . .why you dare to discuss me with my patient's mother?'

'Well, you shouldn't have virtually pushed that poor woman out and closed the door in her face!'

Cindy wished she had spoken to Daniel about this woman ages ago. She didn't need this confrontation today on top of everything else that had happened the last twenty-four hours. Her head and sore body were crying out for her to go and lie down somewhere soft and quiet. She opened her mouth wearily, but then gaped at the sudden transformation on the woman's face and her next words.

Sorrow had swept away the anger, and gentle sympathy oozed from Jennifer as she exclaimed a little too loudly, 'Oh, your poor mother, Dr James. How upset she must be that you are refusing to spend this Christmas with your family when your dad has been so sick and your brother, Ben, has just got engaged! But, then,' she gushed on, 'you're such a very dedicated doctor, aren't you?'

There was a sharp movement behind Cindy and a sharp voice said, 'What's going on out here?' Cindy swung around. Daniel was only a few feet away, looking grimmer than ever.

Before she could speak Jennifer rushed on, 'I was just about to tell her that her sister just rang. At first she didn't want to give me a message, but when Dr James couldn't come to the phone her sister let the cat out of the bag about her family still insisting she go home for Christmas even if it is so busy here.'

And, knowing Naomi, she would only have 'let the cat out of the bag' with considerable help from Jennifer, Cindy fumed. She doubted very much, especially after the warning to herself, that Naomi would have said much to this woman at all so she must be inferring she knew more than she did.

'Naomi rang here?' she exclaimed with a frown. 'I already told her last night I couldn't take any more time off. She should know better than to ring the surgery unless there's an emergency.' She stopped dead at Daniel's angry shake of his head.

'If you wanted to be home with your family on

Christmas Day you should have asked me ages ago,' he snapped. 'Tomorrow's Christmas Eve. Of course it was an urgent call!'

She stared at him with bewilderment. Surely he would understand that she had felt she could not ask him for any more time off until Andrew came home and then, when he had, there just had not really been a chance to speak to Daniel.

Or had there?

With a sense of defeat she knew he was right. She should have asked before this. The truth was simple. Deep down, for the first time in her life and despite even the special circumstances this year, she had not wholeheartedly wanted to be home with her family for Christmas. She had wanted more than anything to enjoy it with Daniel and Brittany.

Daniel suddenly looked very weary. 'Naomi must obviously think it very essential and urgent that you go home if she rang here, then,' he repeated firmly. 'I thought I told you before that we never put important family needs second to our work.'

'I was waiting to see how Andrew was, before requesting Christmas Day off,' she said stiffly.

'There was no need to wait, especially with your father's condition to consider. It could have been arranged last week. Take as much damned time as you like. Tomorrow's Christmas Eve. You can have it off as well as Boxing Day, for all I care!' Daniel slapped the charts in his hand down on Jennifer's desk. 'See to these, please, Jennifer.'

He looked from one woman to the other with a hostile stare. 'I know you two have not been compatible working together. If you can't get your act together one of you will have to leave. I will not tolerate disharmony in this practice. We've enough to put up with at this time of the year,' he snarled, spun on his heel and strode out.

Cindy stared after him blankly and then, completely ignoring the still, pale-faced receptionist, walked back to her room. Blindly she stared down at her clasped hands.

Just like that, it was over.

He didn't even want her working here with him.

With an unnatural calm she forced herself to finish writing up the notes on Amanda. Still calm outwardly, she collected her things. She was thankful Jennifer was nowhere in sight as she left her pile of charts on her desk, before walking blindly out of the medical centre.

Jennifer had worked there for years. In a small place like Sandy Cove capable medical receptionists would not be easy to find. There would be no chance that Daniel's father would agree to her dismissal. Besides, Aileen had already stated she wanted them to find someone to replace her as well. The new kid on the block would be the one who left, especially after that last successful attempt to show up Cindy in such a poor light to Daniel.

That night, after ringing home to tell them she could come after all, Cindy carefully wrapped the presents she had purchased for the Sack family. She would have liked to see Will's dark, flashing eyes as he unwrapped the soft sponge ball and the bat for indoor games. Susan would clutch her new, soft dog and hug it possessively. There was a book of fairy-tales she had hoped Brittany might let her read to her.

When she at last started wrapping the personally engraved gold pen for Daniel her misery intensified.

Like a coward, instead of dropping the gifts over, she rang Aileen, told her she was leaving first thing the next morning and to use the spare key they kept for the flat to pick up the pile of presents for distribution on Christmas morning.

'Would. . .would you tell Daniel and Brittany I wish them a happy Christmas?' she finished in a wooden voice.

Aileen was silent for a moment. 'What a shame. I was hoping we could all have Christmas dinner together. I even bought an extra-big turkey,' she said sadly at last, but added with forced cheerfulness, 'But you'll enjoy being with your family.'

'I. . .I was looking forward to Christmas with you all,' Cindy could not resist saying.

Her voice cracked, and Aileen murmured soothingly something about next year before they finished the call.

And Cindy did enjoy being with her family the next day. She had tried to have a sleep, after hastily packing, but was awake before the sun was up so started home early. The enthusiasm of the welcome-home hugs from her mother and Naomi and the long, thoughtful look at her face by her father before he smiled lovingly and gave her an extra hug as he kissed her gently marginally eased her deep pain.

It was Christmas Eve and she tried her utmost to join cheerfully in the excited, last-moment preparations for the next day. But every now and again Daniel's and his daughter's faces swam across her mind, plunging her into bitter-sweet memories and sadness for what she could have been doing with them tonight.

She slept fitfully and awakened very early to a hot morning that promised that Christmas this year would be a scorcher. Naomi was already in the kitchen, and she put down the phone as Cindy wandered in.

She looked at her with an excited grin. 'Happy Christmas, big sister,' she called gaily, and turned to busy herself with some toast.

Cindy yawned. 'Happy Christmas, Naomi. I hope that wasn't Ben ringing to say he had an emergency and can't make dinner.'

'No, no,' Naomi said quickly. 'Everything's fine. Just an old friend ringing to give me the old Yuletide greetings,' she added flippantly. Her voice was so carefully casual that Cindy smothered a grin. So her baby sister had a secret admirer!

'Good. What time's everyone supposed to get here?'

'Casey's already arrived with his kids from his in-laws' place. He's helping Tom with the milking.'

Both pulled a face at each other. Cows still needed milking even if it was Christmas Day.

Naomi approached the table with a plate of toast dripping with melted butter, talking excitedly the whole time. 'Kim said she was going to sleep in like any heavily pregnant woman was entitled to, especially at Christmas, and that Casey could pick her up before dinner.'

Kim's parents owned a neighbouring property, and Casey and she had always been good friends. It had been so natural for their friendship to progress to love and marriage, Cindy thought wistfully.

She forced her thoughts away from the friendship that had been growing between herself and a tall, dark and handsome man and tried to concentrate on Naomi's chatter.

Tom's wife was coming with their tribe to help with the setting-up of the outdoor patio for the crowd that could no longer fit in the dining room. Ben and Nikki couldn't get there until right on dinnertime.

'But when do we get to open our prezzies?' groaned Cindy.

'Not until after we've eaten,' Naomi said severely, and then gave a burst of giggles. 'You always were the keenest of us all to open presents,' she teased. 'You don't have to worry—there'll be lots of surprises for you, big sis.'

'Yeah, but I still have to wait half a day,' wailed Cindy with mock anguish. She gave a huge sigh and snatched another heavily cholesterol-coated piece of toast. 'I may as well go later on and pick up Kim for Casey.'

Naomi looked thoughtful for a moment and then

excitement lit her eyes. 'A very good idea.' She grinned. 'That way you'll be out of our hair trying to find out which are your parcels under the tree!'

Determinedly Cindy pushed all thoughts of Daniel from her mind. She succeeded quite well all morning until Tom's latest addition to his family toddled in.

James was about the same age as Will. His curls were not as dark, but his cheeky grin beamed at everyone. He suddenly reminded her vividly of the many times she had looked from Will to Daniel and dared to dream about babies of their own, with black bouncing curls and flashing dark eyes.

She stood up hurriedly. 'Time to get the new mother-to-be,' she called brightly.

Only Naomi nodded at her from her position near the drinks table, and thankfully Cindy escaped.

Kim was her usual bouncy self. They chatted cheerfully as they travelled the short distance between the farms.

'Looks like the whole gang's here before me,' Kim said happily as Cindy drove up to the side gate. 'That's Ben's new convertible.' She shook her head. 'He'll have to change his ways when he becomes a sober, married man. Hello, whose is that black car?'

Cindy stopped the car and turned off the ignition, before turning to peer in the direction Kim had indicated.

Her heart nearly stopped. Surely there weren't too many sleek, black cars like. . .like. . .

For a moment she couldn't move.

Kim had already heaved her cumbersome body from the car, and stooped down and looked at Cindy. 'What's up? Come on, I want a drink before we. . . Cindy, what's wrong? You're as white as a sheet.'

Cindy hardly heard her. Her gaze was fixed on the tall, tense figure of the black-haired man approaching with a dancing little replica beside him.

Then her door was flung open. Brittany's gleeful voice shouted, 'Surprise, surprise, Cindy!' and a bundle of warm, loving girl was almost throttling her.

CHAPTER TWELVE

'BRITTANY. . . Daniel. . . What. . .what are you doing here?'

'We decided we wanted to spend Christmas this year with you.' Brittany laughed up at Cindy after another huge hug and kiss.

'Oh, and I did so want to spend it with you,' Cindy said fervently as she kissed and hugged her back.

Then her eyes flew back to Daniel over his daughter's head. He smiled slightly at her, but his eyes were very serious and watchful.

'But the practice. . . Who. . .? How?'

His eyes darkened, he frowned and she knew that once again she had somehow said the wrong thing. He opened his mouth to speak, but Brittany scrambled off Cindy and started hauling her out of the car.

'Oh, Daddy's old friend's looking after that. Do hurry up! Your mother said to tell you to come straight away 'cause everyone's waiting for you.'

Cindy stood up on legs that felt like jelly, unable to take her eyes away from Daniel's beloved face.

His eyes searched hers, and then the hint of a real smile lightened them. 'I'll explain it all to you later,' he murmured gently.

And suddenly joy swept through Cindy as he reached out a hand to take one of hers.

'Happy Christmas, Cindy,' he said simply.

And the next little while or so was very happy.

Cindy felt in a daze. Casey had already introduced Daniel to all her family, and as the voices swelled while they piled up their plates Daniel whispered in her ear,

'Just to set your mind at rest, I found out that an old friend of mine, Scott Campbell, and his wife, Jodi, from Queensland were holidaying in the caravan park. He's looking after the practice today and tomorrow with Andrew's help.' His jaw firmed. 'Even if he hadn't been there I was coming, anyway.'

Tomorrow, too?

Cindy stared at him wide-eyed and then looked quickly away.

She saw Naomi watching them with a smug, knowing expression. 'I told you you'd like at least one of your surprises!' she called across the room.

Cindy flushed as all eyes swung towards her and Daniel. He seemed undisturbed by the attention he had obviously generated the moment he had appeared. As the meal progressed Cindy felt embarrassed as one by one her tall brothers went into their 'checking out Cindy's boyfriend' routine.

However, to her utter relief, Daniel fielded all their questions blandly. Once he caught her watching him and his lips tilted in a sudden warm smile. Instant heat swept through her. Her own lips tilted in response.

She tore her eyes away, suddenly embarrassed that her observant family would notice her making eyes at Daniel. It would not be beyond them to start teasing them mercilessly.

Her gaze collided with Casey's. He looked from her to Daniel and back again with a very serious look on his face. She tilted her chin at him, daring her twin to disapprove of the man she loved.

Then he suddenly winked at her and smiled sweetly. 'Way to go, sis,' he said loudly.

It was their own special twin expression of approval they had used to each other many times over the years, but this time she could have killed him.

There was a choking sound coming from Daniel who

was still standing beside her. She looked at him fearfully, hoping her family was not making him feel too uncomfortable.

Instead, Daniel's face was alight with suppressed laughter. 'I love your twin, too,' he said loudly to Cindy.

Casey gave a loud chortle while Cindy gaped at Daniel for a moment. Then what he had said sunk in and she nearly dropped her plate. A piece of ham slipped off and landed on the ground.

'Cindy, watch what you're doing,' her mother remonstrated crossly, as though she were still an irresponsible teenager.

Cindy looked across the table at her in a daze and then down to where her mother was pointing. Salad dressing was dripping from her sharply tilted plate, and even as she looked a dollop of coleslaw joined the ham.

Yes, she should be watching what she was doing—especially with this infuriating man!

In a very roundabout way, and in front of all her family, had he or had he not just said he loved her?

She rescued her food, forced herself to pick up a knife and fork and headed for one of the chairs scattered around the garden in the shade of the huge gum trees. Suddenly she didn't know whether to laugh or cry as Daniel finished helping himself to a piece of turkey and calmly followed her.

She glared at him, but he just grinned back at her and said blandly, 'I thought you might like to know that Joan Threadgate was admitted to hospital yesterday afternoon.'

Cindy stared at him blankly. Joan Threadgate? She forced herself to think, and then remembered that first day she had gone with him on house calls.

'Oh, the woman with hypertension and pre-toxaemia,' she stammered. 'Is. . .is she all right?'

'Her blood pressure was way up again so I admitted

her and she was fine as soon as her obstetrician did the Caesarean.'

Daniel paused as he filled his mouth with a forkful of turkey. Cindy couldn't take her eyes from his beloved face as he chewed and then glanced up at her.

'She has a healthy baby boy, still a couple of weeks prem but doing fine,' he said conversationally, but with a gleam in his eye.

'That's good,' Cindy murmured, without really thinking about what he was saying, and was relieved when his piercing gaze left her as he turned to answer another query from her nearby father.

Brittany had quickly been roped in to sit with Tom's children and they were busily eating and talking a little distance away. Cindy managed to pick at her food and join in the conversation, and wasn't sure just when she became aware that the children were staring across at her with wide eyes as Brittany held forth.

Her heart sank. She had not mentioned the episode in the surf to any of her family, not even Casey.

'Daniel,' she whispered urgently.

He broke off what he was saying and turned with a raised eyebrow to her. She gestured towards Brittany. He looked over at her for a moment and then back to Cindy with a puzzled frown.

'No one knows about. . .about. . .'

Comprehension filled his face. His lips tightened and he swallowed. Her heart skipped a beat in sudden apprehension.

Oh, Brittany! Why did you have to remind him of my foolishness today?

'You haven't told anybody what happened at the beach, have you, Cindy?'

She stared at him. If anything, he had raised his voice slightly. Her father was watching them curiously.

'Told us what, Cindy?' he asked with interest.

'Dad, it's nothing.'

She shot daggers at Daniel and forced a smile at her father.

Daniel ignored her. He looked down at the fork in his hand. Cindy noticed his hand had clenched on it. Suddenly he put the fork down and reached for a paper serviette. Carefully he wiped his mouth, that beautifully shaped mouth that had kissed her and that she was so hungry for again.

'I thought Jennifer, our receptionist, would have at least told Naomi when she rang the other day.'

He looked up suddenly at Cindy. She was mesmerised, trying to understand the expression on his face.

'Cindy and Brittany went swimming a couple of days ago and were caught in a rip.'

There were exclamations of horror. Daniel ignored them all, never once taking his eyes off Cindy.

'She deliberately swam out to support my daughter until help arrived. It was the bravest and the most terrifying thing I have ever seen. But if she ever puts her life in danger like that again, even for Brittany, I'll personally kill her.'

His reached out and gently stroked a finger down Cindy's cheek. She felt the sudden tremor in it and her own hand reached up and then their fingers were entwined.

Suddenly Daniel looked across at Cindy's father and mother. 'We haven't had a proper talk about it all yet, and I don't think we can wait any longer to do so.'

Everyone went still.

'Why don't you take Daniel for a walk down to the river, Cindy?' her father's calm tones said evenly. 'Take as long as you like, Daniel. We'll watch out for Brittany, but just make sure that when you return that shadow has completely gone from my daughter's face.'

In a daze Cindy looked around at her family. There

were a few sympathetic smiles. Casey mouthed, 'Way to go, Cindy,' again to her.

Then a strong hand had removed the plate she was limply holding in her hand and pulled her to her feet. Silently she let Daniel lead her away on her trembling legs. She vaguely heard the excited chatter and laughter that broke out behind them just before they rounded the corner of the house.

'Your father told me he's doing fine again now, that it was only a temporary setback,' Daniel said softly. 'He's a very brave man, isn't he?'

Still speechless, Cindy tightened her grip on his hand. Her father very rarely mentioned his illness. That he had to Daniel showed how much he must really like him.

'Which way's the river he recommended?'

Cindy looked up at Daniel and she nearly stumbled at the blazing heat in his eyes.

'It's. . .it's beyond the machinery shed. About. . .about five minutes away.'

Daniel stopped dead. 'Is it just? Is your father into torture, then?'

His voice was gruff, unsteady. Then his arms went around her, swinging her against him in a desperate embrace—pressing her full length against his strong but trembling frame.

Cindy clung to him, moulding herself against him. But the comfort of their bodies was not enough. His mouth swept over her face, kissing her forehead, her eyes, her cheeks as though he was desperate to touch every inch of her.

Then he gave a tiny gasp and at last plundered her mouth, his lips pressing against hers in shaking, hungry demand.

Cindy answered his need unstintingly, her own lips parting—allowing him access to all her sweetness until they were both breathless and could only cling together again.

Gradually their trembling eased. Daniel gave a deep, deep sigh.

'Oh, Cindy, girl, I. . .I never dreamt it was possible to feel so. . .so. . .' His scratchy, shaking voice faded away and he clutched her tighter, moving his large hand to press her head against him.

Cindy felt his throat convulse as he swallowed. With her face still tucked into his neck, she smiled slightly. For perhaps the first time in his life this strong, assertive man was lost for words.

Very gently she moved until she could stare up into his eyes and then she reluctantly pushed away from him.

'Daniel. . .' she began huskily, and stopped, not sure where to start.

He took a deep breath, pulled her back into his arms for a quick hug as though he couldn't not be touching her and then reluctantly let her go.

'I know,' he said with a wry grin, 'I've got a bit of explaining to do.'

Cindy's gaze darkened. 'That you have, Daniel Burston. Like why you could hardly bear to even look at me after—'

'I know, I know,' he interrupted her and looked around uneasily. 'We could have members of your family, particularly the smaller fry, run around here at any time. Perhaps we'd better find that river if we want any peace.'

It took much longer than five minutes before they reached the shade of the tall gum trees along the banks of the river. Several magpies warbled in their branches, and Cindy thought it must be the most beautiful place on earth. Every few steps Daniel had stolen another kiss 'to make up for all those we've missed out on already,' as he put it.

'Who's complaining?' Cindy growled smartly, and in

one of her favourite spots beside the slowly flowing water she pulled him around to plant several kisses on his strong throat.

He groaned. 'Dr James, if you don't stop this I'm likely to go into cardiac failure worse than ever.'

She laughed up at him. 'Serves you right, Dr Burston, for being such a pain.'

He studied her loving, bewitching face and lost his own smile. 'I have been incredibly stupid, haven't I?'

She put her head cheekily on one side. 'Well, now,' she drawled, 'if I knew exactly which incident you were referring to I'd know whether to agree or not.'

But he remained serious. A shadow crossed his face, and Cindy could not bear the sudden anguish that filled his beloved eyes.

'The longest stupidity has been with Brittany. We talked for a long time last night.'

'Oh, she told you about her fear of not being able to remember her mother.'

'That and then. . .' he smiled tenderly at her '. . .she raved on and on about this wonderful woman named Cindy who, according to what she claimed, should really be sporting a halo and wings at least. I agreed with her, and she demanded to know why I had let you go home without the pair of us. I found myself agreeing, and here we are,' he finished simply.

Cindy's eyes went a little misty. She returned the squeeze of his hands and then withdrew them as she chose her words carefully.

'She really could remember very few times with her mother, Daniel.'

'That's because Sally never did spend much time with her daughter at all.'

Cindy remained silent, waiting.

Daniel looked around and then moved over to a patch of thick grass and sat down, patting the grass invitingly beside him. Cindy curled up next to him and he took her hand, frowning down at it as he held it between both of his.

'Sally never really wanted a family. She only had Brittany because she knew how much I wanted a child, and our marriage was already in trouble.' He sighed. 'In hindsight, she was probably a woman who should never have married. I certainly found that even I came a very poor second to her precious career,' he added with a trace of bitterness.

'And yet you started a general practice together?'

Daniel's face twisted. 'And that was a compromise. As I told you before, she and Dad didn't get on. Sally knew when we married that I wanted to return to Sandy Cove and work with my father and Andrew. After we were married she told me bluntly it was too far away from Sydney for all the committees and extra training courses she wanted to be involved in. She was a good mother to Brittany that first year, although I did wonder sometimes if even that was only so she could claim to have hands-on experience for her career. After that she became even more wrapped up in promoting women's health issues.'

He moved restlessly. 'The trouble was there was no argument that there was desperate need for her expertise in the area we lived in. My argument was that she did not have to try and do it all herself, and at the expense of her relationship with her husband and daughter.'

He looked up and studied Cindy's face. He lifted a hand and tenderly smoothed a swathe of her golden hair from her forehead.

'And then along comes an incredibly beautiful woman who simply took my breath away, someone I was attracted to even when I thought she was the babysitter.'

Cindy gave a low chuckle and he smiled at her.

'The problem was I had vowed that if ever I did

contemplate marrying anyone it would never be another doctor, especially one who could put her family a long way second to her career and patients.'

Cindy reached up and in turn ran her hand gently over his face. He turned his head and captured her palm with his kiss.

'Daniel, you've heard me talk about my family, and now you've met them *en masse*. Do you think I could really grow up in that family-orientated atmosphere and not know what value to put on any family I might have of my own?'

He was silent for a moment and then gave a quick shake of his head in agreement. His mouth opened but Cindy quickly put her hand on his lips.

'My turn for a moment,' she said firmly.

She paused and once again carefully chose her words. It was so important that she convinced him that her priorities were the same as his although, with the depth of his hurt, probably only years of working, living and loving together with this wonderful man would really convince him.

'This is one area where you've been very blind, even stupid, if you like. Surely to goodness the mere fact that I was so prepared to stay in Aileen's and Andrew's house with you because of the children should have told you I was nothing like Sally!'

He looked at her seriously for a moment, and then amusement filled his eyes. 'I must confess that at first I thought you only stayed because I'd really given you very little choice.'

Cindy raised her chin but a long finger reached out and pressed it down. 'I know, I know, you're not such a weak wimp as all that.'

She looked at him dangerously. 'Weak wimp?'

He grinned at her and then stilled. There was a fleeting touch of pain and he closed his eyes for a moment. She watched him quietly and started to pull her hand from his. His grip tightened and he looked at her.

'I'm so sorry, Daniel,' she whispered.

He frowned suddenly. 'Sorry? About what?' His face cleared. 'Oh, you mean that row you had with Jennifer?'

That wasn't what she had meant at all, but apparently he thought she had some need to apologise for that as well.

He quickly disillusioned her by the two short, sharp words he used to describe cattle manure and Jennifer Coats in the same breath.

She scowled disapprovingly. 'You really do need to make sure you don't swear where Brittany can hear you, Daniel. She knows enough swear words as it is!'

He merely scowled right back. 'Well, that woman would make anyone swear.'

Cindy was inclined to agree with him but bit her tongue.

'You don't have to worry about her any longer. She resigned this morning.'

Distressed, Cindy opened her mouth but he raised a hand. 'I knew from your first day she resented you for some reason.'

Cindy thought of Naomi's shrewd comments, but chose to remain silent.

'I nearly sacked her on the spot when she informed me in that first week, in front of Brittany, too, that you were not suitable for the practice but I had been thinking of suggesting to her that she resign even before you came on the scene. I don't know how Dad never caught her out but the woman has a gossiping tongue,' he said grimly. 'Too many patients were telling me things about other patients they could only have heard from one of us or our receptionist.'

Cindy knew that only too well, she thought grimly.

She looked up at Daniel to find him studying her

thoughtfully. 'But I don't think you were referring to Jennifer, were you, sweetheart?'

Numbly she shook her head. 'Oh, my darling, I should never have taken Brittany to the beach that day. I'm sorry I made you so angry with me. I'll never forgive myself for risking her life the way I—'

'Risking her life? You nearly lost yours, trying to save the little monkey!'

There was a return of some of the fury that had haunted her ever since seeing his rage on the beach.

'But. . .but you were so angry with me,' she pleaded helplessly.

'With you?' He sucked in a quick breath. 'I'm not sure who I was angry with—those lifesavers who should have been still on duty or fate that had threatened to take away from me the two people I loved the most in all the world.'

He gave a wry smile. 'Now I know why people suffer from the unreasonable anger of relief that sometimes comes when a loved one is safe at last.'

He reached over and convulsively pulled her into his arms, holding her tightly as though he would guard and keep her from anything that could possibly harm and separate them.

'The only thing you have to be sorry about, so sorry I hope you never ever dare do it again, is for risking your precious life!'

Cindy was stunned as his strong body began to tremble in her arms.

'When I arrived home and Aileen was full of delight because you had left that message that you were together I raced off to the beach to join you.'

Cindy's eyes widened, suddenly realising that was why he had been there.

'I had hardly parked the car when someone yelled out to me that the boat had gone out to a woman and a kid caught in a rip,' Daniel continued in clipped tones. 'The man said they were a long way out. There was doubt they would be able to stay afloat long enough for the boat to reach them. They'd undoubtedly need me.'

Daniel closed his eyes momentarily. 'And I knew...'

'Oh, Daniel,' Cindy whispered in horror.

He shuddered. 'It was the longest, most horrible moment of my life.'

Then his hands encircled her face and he looked intently into her eyes, his still dark with the remembered terror of those ghastly moments.

'It was an accident, pure and simple, but it terrified the daylights out of me. I've already lost someone I loved. Losing Sally made me very sad for a long time, but I suddenly wasn't sure if I could survive losing you. So, like the prize idiot I am, I tried very hard not to love you.'

She felt the sudden tremor in his hands. 'That day I didn't want to love you! It hurt too damned much! You were already so shocked and shaken. I was afraid to touch you and kiss you the way I longed to in case I couldn't let you go.'

Sudden memory of the anguish she had felt at his withdrawal from her swept over her. With a burst of strength, Cindy pushed him away and sprang to her feet. She glared at him furiously. He stared at her with surprise and then slowly stood up also.

'You were right,' she yelled at him. 'You really are a stupid, stupid man! For heaven's sake, I had just fought the darned ocean and won! Did you think I was made of sugar and spice and would dissolve if you touched me? I needed you! I needed you to grab me and—'

'Like this, do you mean?' he yelled back, his eyes blazing.

He hauled her into his arms so strongly that they both stumbled on the uneven ground. Cindy felt the smooth, cool wood of a gum tree against her back and leaned against it as she hung desperately onto this infuriating man.

'All right, I did blame you!' Daniel gave her a little shake. 'Like on that very first day when I found myself using all kinds of excuses to keep you in the same house, even when my dear sister stated she didn't mind staying home herself so you and Naomi could go.'

Cindy's eyes widened indignantly.

'I blamed you for being such a wonderful person that any man with an ounce of sense could not help falling in love with you,' he continued furiously.

'I blamed you for all kinds of stupid irrational things because I was so desperately in love with you, and scared witless that you had nearly drowned, and scared you wouldn't want to take on a ready-made family of one eight-year-old girl who had been horrible to you, and scared you wouldn't want to join our Sandy Cove practice permanently, or to marry a man who isn't the least bit ambitious—just happy to be a family doctor in a small town for the rest of his life.'

All her dreams were within her grasp. Cindy froze.

Daniel felt her go still in his arms and pushed her away so he could stare anxiously into her eyes.

Cindy stared back at him. His face went a little pale and he let her go, taking a step back.

Good, let him suffer—

No, she loved him too much, but there were some things a woman had a right to—like a proper declaration of love and a decent proposal!

She put her hands on her hips. 'Daniel Burston, you have not yet actually told me directly that you love me, and have not yet directly asked me to marry you.'

Her eyes narrowed. 'You've just admitted you didn't even want to love me.'

Cindy held her breath as he stared at her. Then a

wonderful light flooded his face, sweeping away his confusion and anxiety and filling his face with such tenderness and love that as his lips descended to hers again an answering fire began to surge through Cindy.

'Da-a-ddy. . .!'

They both swung towards the house. A tribe of children was descending on them, led by a frantically waving Brittany.

'Uncle Casey said you should be finished all that by now and we can't wait any longer to open our presents!'

Daniel and Cindy looked at each other. They laughed.

Then Daniel was serious again. 'I love you very much, Dr James.'

'Da-a-ddy. . .!'

'And would you please marry me, my darling?' he finished in a rush.

Cindy smiled contentedly and caressed his face gently, lovingly, amazed that it was possible to feel so deliriously happy.

'I love you very much too, Dr Burston, and I fully intend to marry you as soon as possible.'

Suddenly she spun around and put both hands around her mouth. 'Brittany,' she yelled exuberantly, 'go tell everybody you're going to have a new mother and they can start on the presents without us! I've already got all I need right here!'

Brittany beamed from ear to ear and let out a whoop. She held her clenched hands above her head in a victory salute and headed for the house, yelling the news for all to hear.

Daniel and Cindy grinned at each other again. Then Daniel sighed.

'Well, I suppose we had better get used to being interrupted with that young miss around.'

'And with all the other, curly-headed children, especially if there are twins,' Cindy whispered.

'All the other. . .?'

Cindy beamed at the bemused look on her love's face. His expression suddenly changed to startled, blissful comprehension.

She pulled him close once again. Then their lips met with such love and passion, sealing their love and commitment to each other, that it was a long time before they thought of anything so mundane as the other Christmas gifts awaiting them.

PARTY TIME!

How would you like to win a year's supply of Mills & Boon® Books? Well, you can and they're FREE! Simply complete the competition below and send it to us by 31st August 1998. The first five correct entries picked after the closing date will each win a year's subscription to the Mills & Boon series of their choice. What could be easier?

BALLOONS
STREAMER
DRINKS
MUSIC
BUFFET
DANCING
CELEBRATE
PARTIES
ENTERTAIN
INVITE
FANCY DRESS
HANGOVER

S	O	E	T	A	R	B	E	L	E	C
T	E	F	M	U	S	I	C	D	D	H
S	U	I	V	Z	T	E	Y	R	A	A
N	E	N	T	E	R	T	A	I	N	N
O	B	V	E	R	E	H	K	N	C	G
O	J	I	F	O	A	L	R	K	I	O
L	M	T	F	V	M	P	U	S	N	V
L	P	E	U	Q	E	N	Z	S	G	E
A	W	G	B	X	R	C	T	B	Y	R
B	F	A	N	C	Y	D	R	E	S	S

C8B

Please turn over for details of how to enter...

HOW TO ENTER

Can you find our twelve party words? They're all hidden somewhere in the grid. They can be read backwards, forwards, up, down or diagonally. As you find each word in the grid put a line through it. When you have completed your wordsearch, don't forget to fill in the coupon below, pop this page into an envelope and post it today—you don't even need a stamp!

Mills & Boon Party Time! Competition
FREEPOST CN81, Croydon, Surrey, CR9 3WZ
EIRE readers send competition to PO Box 4546, Dublin 24.

Please tick the series you would like to receive if you are one of the lucky winners

Presents™ ❑ Enchanted™ ❑ Medical Romance™ ❑
Historical Romance™ ❑ Temptation® ❑

Are you a Reader Service™ Subscriber? Yes ❑ No ❑

Mrs/Ms/Miss/Mr ....Intials ....
(BLOCK CAPITALS PLEASE)

Surname..

Address ....

....

.....................................Postcode.........................

(I am over 18 years of age)

C8B

One application per household. Competition open to residents of the UK and Ireland only. You may be mailed with offers from other reputable companies as a result of this application. If you would prefer not to receive such offers, please tick box. ❑

Closing date for entries is 31st August 1998.